THE
HEX
FACTOR

Harriet Goodwin

Stripes

1.
Art

"It's no use hiding behind that pile of books!" said Mr Wood, smiling across the classroom at Xanthe. "I know you're there!" He checked the register. "And since you're the only person who hasn't spoken yet, I'm guessing you must be Xanthe Fox. What an unusual name!"

Xanthe turned crimson.

"So come on, then, Xanthe. It's your turn to tell me a bit about yourself."

Xanthe fiddled with the zip on her pencil case, trawling her mind for a suitable excuse. If there was one thing she hated it was speaking in front of the whole class. She just couldn't stand all those pairs of eyes on her. She glanced across the table at her best friend, Grace, who shot her a sympathetic look in return.

Mr Wood cleared his throat. "I'll be standing in for Mrs Atkins for the rest of the year, you see," he said. "And as a new member of staff I need to get to know you all as quickly as possible. This is the best way I can think of doing it." He picked up his notebook. "Tell me about your family, Xanthe. Do you have any brothers and sisters?"

Xanthe shook her head.

"Pets?"

"No," replied Xanthe. "I had a kitten once, but Dad was allergic to it, so we had to give it away."

Mr Wood nodded sympathetically and leaned back in his chair. "What about school? What subjects are you good at?"

Xanthe hesitated.

It was hard to know what to say, really. She was just about OK at English and history, but she wasn't exactly *good* at them. And when it came to subjects like maths and science she seriously struggled.

"Come on, Xanthe! You're among friends. It's not as if you're new, like Donna here." He gestured towards a slim, pale-faced girl sitting some distance away from Xanthe. "You don't need to say much. A couple of sentences will do fine. Just something for me to try and remember you by."

"I – I like art," murmured Xanthe. "I wish we had it every day."

"She won a prize for it, sir," called out a fair-headed boy from the other side of the classroom. "Every year the head gives out a trophy at Prize Night for someone whose work has really stood out. He picks one person from the whole school, and last year it was Xanthe."

Xanthe blushed again and gave the boy a shy smile.

"Fantastic!" said Mr Wood, his eyes flitting over the register. "Thank you for that, Saul." He scribbled something in his notebook. "Why do you like art so much, Xanthe? What makes it special for you?"

Xanthe thought for a moment. From her place at the back of the classroom she could just make out the corner of the art block through the window. She'd be in there later today, and she couldn't wait.

"It's hard to explain," she said, running her fingers through her short chestnut hair. "All I know is that when I've got a paintbrush in my hand I kind of lose myself. It's like I forget where I am and who I am and something just takes over. The lines and the shapes and the colours seem to appear on the paper as if they were there inside me all the time, waiting to get out…"

She broke off.

"Sorry," she mumbled. "That sounds really stupid."

Mr Wood stood up and came round to the front

of his desk. "Not at all," he said. "That was excellent, Xanthe. I don't think anyone's spoken with so much enthusiasm all morning. Never lose that passion. It sounds like art is what you've been born to do."

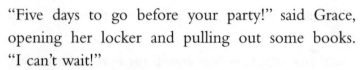

"Five days to go before your party!" said Grace, opening her locker and pulling out some books. "I can't wait!"

Xanthe grinned. "Neither can I! Did I tell you Mum had a call from that DJ? You know, the one Pippa had for her thirteenth? He's had a cancellation, so he's coming on Saturday night."

"Oh wow!" exclaimed Grace. "That is so cool!"

Saul turned round from his locker. "Don't you two talk about anything else?" he said, grinning. "Thanks for texting me about that gig, by the way, Xanthe. I'm definitely going to try and get tickets."

A girl with long blonde hair pushed past them on her way to her locker. "I bet you're pleased with yourself," she said, flicking back her hair and scowling at Xanthe. "Getting into Mr Wood's good books like that. Honestly, it was enough to make anyone throw up."

Xanthe sighed. "I wasn't looking for praise, Kelly. I was just answering his question, that's all."

Saul glared at Kelly.

"First day of the new term and you're already showing your true colours," he said. "And all because you're *still* jealous of Xanthe winning that trophy last year. It's pathetic." He moved to one side so that the new girl could reach her locker. "Anyway, what Xanthe said was way better than *your* little speech." He flicked back his hair in a perfect impression of Kelly. *"Hi. I'm Kelly. I absolutely love school. I'm top in maths and science and last term I got to sign the Book of Excellence three times!"*

Beside him Grace burst out laughing.

Kelly narrowed her eyes and stormed off, knocking into Xanthe as she went.

"You shouldn't have done that," said Xanthe, shaking her head at Saul.

"Well, someone needs to tell her," said Saul. "That was well out of order."

"I know you were just sticking up for me, but − well − you know what she's like. She'll really have it in for me now, won't she? You too, if you're not careful."

Saul snorted. "Kelly Snier doesn't scare me. And she shouldn't scare you, either. She's just jealous. Anyway, she's all mouth and no action."

He looked across at the new girl, who was struggling to open her locker. "Here," he said, holding out his hand for her key. "Donna, isn't it? D'you want me to have a go? There's a bit of a knack to them."

Donna blushed and handed Saul the key.

"Thanks," she said.

"Sorry about all that just now," said Saul, jiggling the key from side to side. "Though you might as well get used to it. Kelly's had it in for Xanthe since last summer. And by the looks of it, nothing's about to change."

"I wish she'd get over it," sighed Xanthe. "There's no *need* to be jealous of me. She's miles better at everything than I am. She's probably the cleverest student in the year. Still, Saul's right. It's all just snide comments with Kelly. She never actually *does* anything. She's too scared of getting on the wrong side of the teachers."

Donna glanced from Saul to Xanthe, but said nothing.

"There you go!" said Saul, standing back as the locker door swung open at last. He flashed Donna a wide smile and handed her back the key. "Just give me a shout if you need it doing again."

"Thanks," murmured Donna. "Thanks a lot." She watched as Saul picked up his bag and sauntered off with a group of boys. Then she grabbed some books out of her locker, closed it behind her and scuttled down the corridor after them.

"She seems very shy, doesn't she?" said Grace,

when Donna was out of earshot. "Still, I guess it can't be easy changing schools partway through the year, and then being asked to speak in front of the whole class on your first day." She waited while Xanthe finished getting her books. "I can't actually remember what she said. Something about moving to the area because of her dad's new job, wasn't it? Oh, and liking art, too. You should try getting to know her, Xanthe. It sounds like you two have something in common."

"Yeah, maybe," said Xanthe, nodding absently. She rooted around inside her bag. "What've we got after break? I can't find my timetable."

"Double science," replied Grace. "Your favourite!"

Xanthe groaned. She linked arms with Grace and together they set off down the corridor.

It looked like it was going to be a tedious morning, but at least she had something to look forward to. After lunch it was art.

"Our focus this term," said Miss Evans, rolling up the sleeves of her blouse and smiling round at the assembled students, "is on portraying human expressions."

She twisted her hair into a loose knot on top of her head.

"We're going to be using all sorts of different mediums. Charcoal, watercolour, acrylics. We might even have a go with oils if we have time. Today, though, we're going to get back to basics. I've filled four pots on each table with poster paints. Nice bright colours to stimulate your imaginations. Reds and greens and blues and yellows. And I want you to use them to portray some of the big human emotions. Joy. Sadness. Anger. That sort of thing. We'll leave the subtler feelings till later in the term."

Xanthe breathed in the familiar smell of the art room. After the torture of double science, this was bliss. Everywhere she looked there was artwork: landscapes; seascapes; portraits. Some of it was quite basic stuff the Year Sevens had done last term. But there was Sixth Form work, too, including some amazing sketches by Jenny Adamson, one of the Upper Sixth girls who had left last year to take up a scholarship at the Slade School of Art. According to Miss Evans, Jenny was the best artist the school had ever had.

She sighed. If she ever won a scholarship to the Slade she reckoned she'd be the happiest person alive. She gazed at the pots on the tables in front of them, her fingers twitching in her eagerness to start painting.

Miss Evans smiled at her. "I can see some of you are dying to get going." She glanced down at the register. "I'm going to pair you up with someone you haven't worked with before. And while you're waiting to start, I'd like you to think about the various expressions we use. You'll really need to *feel* the emotion you want your partner to portray."

She began calling out names and directing people to tables.

Xanthe watched as Grace was paired off with Alex Macpherson and Saul was seated at a table near the back with Donna. Knowing her luck she'd get put with Simon Morris or one of the Cooper twins: someone who'd mess about all lesson and refuse to take things seriously.

"Xanthe," said Miss Evans, "I want you to work with Kelly. You paint her first, then swap after twenty minutes. I'll be coming round the classroom to see how you're getting on."

Xanthe's heart sank. She'd been waiting all day for art, and now it was about to be ruined by Kelly Snier. From the other side of the room, Grace rolled her eyes. Xanthe shrugged in response, then took her place at the table opposite Kelly and reached for a brush. She'd just have to concentrate on the task in hand. She didn't actually have to talk to Kelly, did she? She only had to paint her.

"So, how's it going, then, *Picasso*?" hissed Kelly across the table. She needled Xanthe with her ice-cold blue eyes.

Xanthe said nothing. She dipped the brush in the jar of red paint and forced herself to study the expression on Kelly's mouth. What was it on those thin lips she could see exactly? Jealousy? Hatred? Scorn? A mixture of all three, most probably. Well, it was going to take more than a splash of poster paint to capture an expression like that.

She wiped the excess paint on to the rim of the jar.

"Sweet of your boyfriend to stick up for you earlier," Kelly went on. "Even if he *is* a complete loser."

"He is *not* a loser," muttered Xanthe, the colour rising in her cheeks. "And he's not my boyfriend, either. He's just…"

"A good friend?" supplied Kelly. She smirked. "That's what you always say. Well, I think it might be a bit more than that." She slid one hand across the table and began to twist the pot of red poster paint round and round.

Xanthe pretended not to notice. She pursed her lips, concentrating on the exact curve of Kelly's mouth.

The pot was still turning, the red paint slopping around inside it.

"Can you stop doing that, please?" muttered Xanthe.

Kelly took no notice. "Always the little artist," she said softly. "Always Miss Evans's favourite."

"I am not Miss Evans's favourite. She doesn't *have* favourites."

Miss Evans approached and Kelly slipped her hand neatly into her lap.

"How are you doing, girls? I see you've chosen a rather complicated emotion to portray, Xanthe. How would you describe it exactly?"

Xanthe flushed.

"I-I don't know," she stammered. "I'm just painting what I can see."

Miss Evans beamed at her. "Good, good," she said. "Precisely what I want to hear!" She turned away towards the next table.

"Precisely what I want to hear!" mimicked Kelly, putting on a sickly smile and batting her eyelids. "See what I mean? You can't put a foot wrong, can you?" Her hand crept back across the table and the paint pot started to twist again.

Xanthe reached out to steady it … and the next moment its entire contents was arching through the air in a brilliant red curve, landing with a wet slap all over the back of Miss Evans's white cotton blouse.

Kelly jumped to her feet.

"Xanthe!" she exclaimed, her face a perfect study of shock and horror. "How *could* you?"

Xanthe sat motionless at the table, the empty paint pot in her hand, watching as rivulets of bright red paint trickled down Miss Evans's blouse – and knowing without even looking that everyone was staring straight at her.

2.
Grandma Alice

"How could Miss Evans even *think* it was me?" cried Xanthe, turning to Grace as the class trooped out of the art block at the end of the afternoon. "She knows how much I love art. I'd never do a thing like that."

"Lucky for you she likes you so much," said Saul, coming up behind them. "No one else would've got off so lightly." He grinned. "I guess that'll be the last time she puts you and Kelly together."

Xanthe frowned. "It's not funny, Saul! I could've been in serious trouble. It's a miracle she didn't send me to Mr Maguire. Anyway, that's not the point. The *point* is, she didn't believe me when I told her it wasn't my fault. I can't explain *how* Kelly did it, but somehow she made that paint land on Miss Evans.

She did it to get me in trouble."

Grace put an arm round her.

"Calm down, Xanthe," she said. "*We* believe you. But you've got to be realistic. It didn't exactly look good, did it? You were the one holding the empty paint pot – and nobody else actually saw what happened."

Saul nodded. "Yeah, I was busy painting Donna." He led the way into the main school building. "She was very quiet at the beginning of the lesson. Looked like she was miles away. But later on she opened up quite a bit. In fact, she was really friendly. And her picture of me was pretty good, too, so you'd better watch out this term, Xanthe!"

"What about Kelly, though?" said Xanthe impatiently. "Why d'you think she's suddenly decided to cause trouble? She's never done anything like this before."

Saul shrugged. "Let it go. Going over it like this won't help. Just be pleased Miss Evans didn't give you a detention." He checked his watch. "I've got to go. I've got a drum lesson, and Mr Hurst'll kill me if I'm late. See you tomorrow."

The two girls watched as he hurried off down the corridor.

"He's right," said Grace. "You're better off forgetting all about it." She glanced at Xanthe. "Tell you what, why don't we go down to the park before it gets dark? I'll buy you a hot chocolate in the café."

Xanthe shook her head. "Thanks, but I don't really feel like it. Besides, I told Grandma Alice I'd drop in on her after school today. I haven't seen her since Christmas and I owe her a visit."

"Oh, come on! It'll cheer you up."

Xanthe gave a small smile. "Another time. I'm just not in the mood right now. I'll try and cheer up, though, I promise."

Grace sighed.

"You better had," she said. "It's your birthday tomorrow, remember. And your party at the weekend." She started up the stairs towards the lockers. "Come on, let's get our things and I'll walk with you to your bus stop. You don't want to keep your great-grandma waiting."

Xanthe waved goodbye to Grace and stepped on to the bus.

She made her way to the back, ignoring the stares and whispers from some of the other students. It looked like her classmates had done a pretty good job of spreading the word already. By tomorrow the whole school would probably know what had happened in art that afternoon.

She sat down and put her bag on the floor. It hadn't exactly been a great start to the term, had it? She'd been told off in front of the entire class. And for something she hadn't even done.

Worse still, she had upset Miss Evans.

She shuddered at the memory of her favourite teacher splattered with red paint. *What a disappointment.* That's what she'd said. *Letting yourself down like that on the first day back. I would never have expected such childish behaviour from you.* She could still hear the words ringing in her ears.

She willed herself not to cry.

Kelly had had it in for her for months now. Whether it was a race on the sports field or some minor triumph in a lesson, her classmate could always be relied on to crush her achievements with some horrible comment. But she'd never actually *done* anything before. She'd always been too scared of getting into trouble.

As the bus pulled away from Milchester High and rumbled off into the grey January afternoon, Xanthe rested her head against the window.

It must have been the praise from Mr Wood that had tipped Kelly over the edge. That, and Saul bringing up Prize Night in front of everyone. He shouldn't have had a go at Kelly beside the lockers, either. It had been nice of him to stick up for her – but didn't he realize how much worse it made everything?

She cringed at the thought of what her mum and dad would say. Perhaps she wouldn't tell them – at least, not yet. Not with her birthday tomorrow and her party at the weekend. There was no point in spoiling things, was there? And she wouldn't say anything to Grandma Alice, either. Usually she told her great-grandmother everything, but this was just too embarrassing.

Xanthe got to her feet as her stop came into view. Picking up her bag, she made her way to the doors at the front of the bus.

For the next few hours, she was going to put on a brave face.

Xanthe rounded the corner to Hawthorne Close and stopped outside number twenty-two. She unlatched the gate and stood for a moment looking at her great-grandmother's front garden.

It was as bare as ever. Mrs Batley, who lived next door, had planted her little patch with snowdrops and aconites, and in another few weeks it would be a perfect rectangle of white and yellow flowers.

Xanthe clicked her tongue.

She had *tried* to get Grandma Alice interested in

the garden. Even if her great-grandmother was too frail to do much in it, at least she could have enjoyed the view. Last autumn she'd even bought her a couple of packets of bulbs and offered to plant them for her. But the old lady had just glanced down at the packets and pulled one of her faces. *What would I want with a garden?* she'd asked. *I'd have to keep it tidy, wouldn't I? I don't have the time, Xanthe, dear. I simply don't have the time.*

I don't have the time. That was what her great-grandmother always said. According to her, she didn't have time for gardening or knitting or needlework or anything else other people's grandmas seemed to enjoy. Well, as far as Xanthe could see, Grandma Alice had plenty of time. She just didn't put it to very good use, that was all. Even for someone of her age, being stuck indoors watching back-to-back soaps and period dramas didn't seem like much of a life.

The front door swung open and Grandma Alice held out her arms to greet her. Dressed in a purple twinset and with her short grey hair neatly combed, she looked as smart as ever, though her tiny frame seemed a little more hunched than usual.

"Hello, sweetheart!" she exclaimed, beaming at Xanthe. "How wonderful to see you!"

Xanthe hurried down the path towards her.

"Sorry I haven't been round sooner," she said, hugging her great-grandmother. "It's been manic since Christmas."

"You mean you had better things to do than pass the time with an ancient old crone like me!" teased Grandma Alice. "Don't look so shocked – I don't blame you one bit!" She beckoned Xanthe inside. "Come on in. I've got a lemon drizzle cake for tea."

Xanthe frowned. "You haven't been out to the shops, have you?" she said. "You know what the district nurse told you, Grandma. You need to rest your hip for a fortnight. No sneaky trips out."

Her great-grandmother scowled. "Yes, Dr Xanthe. I remember exactly what she said. And if you reckon I'm going to take a blind bit of notice of that bossy woman, you've got another think coming." She sniffed. "But no, for your information I haven't been out. Your mother did a shop for me at the weekend. *Satisfied?*"

Xanthe nodded, laughing. "Satisfied!" She followed Grandma Alice down a short corridor and into a tiny sitting room, furnished with a rose-patterned three-piece suite, a walnut bureau and an ancient cuckoo clock.

"Make yourself at home," said her great-grandmother. "I'll go and put the kettle on and dig out that cake."

Xanthe sat down in one of the armchairs, smiling as a white cat with bright blue eyes leaped up beside her and curled itself into a soft heap in her lap. "Hello, Blanche," she said. "Go on, snuggle up. I could do with a cuddle right now." She stroked the cat's silky ears and sighed. Sitting here in the warm fug of Grandma Alice's sitting room, she could almost believe this afternoon hadn't happened.

A minute or two later, her great-grandmother came shuffling into the room, carrying a tray.

"Now then," she said, when at last they were sitting opposite one another, nursing cups of tea and slices of cake. "Are you going to tell me what's up?"

Xanthe flushed. "What d'you mean?"

Her great-grandmother sipped her tea. "Oh, come on, Xanthe, I saw you standing beside my gate just now. You had a face like thunder. It doesn't take a genius to work out something's bothering you."

Xanthe bowed her head. "Is it really that obvious?" she muttered. "I wasn't going to say anything."

Grandma Alice laughed. "You can't keep secrets from me. You should know that by now." She took a bite of cake. "Surely your first day back at school can't have been that bad?"

Xanthe picked at the lemony crust on top of her cake. "Yes, it was," she said. "It was the worst day *ever*."

Her great-grandmother looked at her shrewdly. "Kelly Snier?"

Xanthe nodded.

Grandma Alice gestured towards the cake in Xanthe's hand.

"Three mouthfuls," she instructed. "Three whole mouthfuls before you utter another word. There's nothing so bad a bit of lemon drizzle won't make better. Then you can tell me all about it."

Xanthe grinned in spite of herself. She bit into her cake, closing her eyes as its sweet sharpness flooded her tastebuds. She took a second bite, then a third, before wiping the crumbs from her mouth and settling back in her armchair.

"It started all right," she said. "We've got this new form teacher – Mr Wood. He's standing in for Mrs Atkins while she's on maternity leave." She rested her hand on Blanche's fur. "He wanted to get to know us, so we each had to say something about ourselves."

"I can't imagine you enjoyed that. What did you say?"

"It wasn't so bad, actually. I told him about art and how it makes me feel, and when I'd finished he said I'd done really well. But afterwards Kelly was snide about what I'd said, and Saul overheard and pretty much told her to get lost."

"And then what happened?" asked Grandma Alice.

She picked up the teapot, her mole-flecked hand shaking a little as she poured herself another cup of tea.

Xanthe's face clouded. "We were in art after lunch. We had to work in pairs and Miss Evans put me with Kelly. She started messing about with a pot of red paint on our table and before I knew it there was paint all over Miss Evans and I was getting the blame."

"So Kelly made it look like you'd done it?"

"Exactly. She obviously wanted to get back at me for what Saul had said. But this time it wasn't just snide comments I had to deal with. *Amazingly*, Miss Evans decided not to report me to Mr Maguire, but she still gave me a massive telling-off in front of everyone."

Grandma Alice took a sip of tea. "Poor old Xanthe," she said. "You *have* had a bad day." She put down her cup and saucer. "Still, it could have been worse. At least Miss Evans didn't report you. And look on the bright side – it's your birthday tomorrow. A very special one, too. You only get to be thirteen once in your life."

Xanthe nodded glumly. "I s'pose…"

"I think you'll find I've marked the occasion with an especially nice gift. Something small but special. I've given it to your mother with strict instructions not to hand it over till the morning."

Xanthe looked up. "But aren't you coming to my birthday dinner? Can't you give it to me then?"

Grandma Alice shook her head. "You said yourself I'm not to venture out, not even round the corner to yours. And getting in and out of the car is agony."

"Couldn't we come to you? Have the birthday dinner here?"

Her great-grandmother smiled. "That's sweet of you, Xanthe. Your mother suggested the same thing. But I'd rather no one made a fuss on my account." She leaned forwards in her chair. "In any case, what I'd really like is for you to come over by yourself the day after and have a special celebration tea – just you and me. There are two parts to your present, you see, and I thought if you came over on Wednesday, I could give you the second part in person."

"Two parts to my present?" echoed Xanthe. "That sounds intriguing! Oh, Grandma! You can't say all that and not tell me what it is…"

Grandma Alice gave her a mischievous grin. "When you get to my age you can do exactly what you like!"

The doorbell rang and she pulled herself to her feet. "That'll be the district nurse come to check up on me," she groaned. "D'you want to stay for a bit and help me get rid of her?"

Xanthe laughed. "No, thanks. I'd better get going." She set Blanche down on the floor and reached for her bag. "I told Mum I wouldn't be late, and I've got a stack of homework already."

Her great-grandmother nodded. "Till Wednesday, then?" she said, leading the way back down the corridor. "You'll come round for tea after school?"

Xanthe settled her bag on her shoulder and dropped a kiss on her great-grandmother's papery cheek.

"Of course I will," she said. "I wouldn't miss it for the world."

3.
Thirteen

Xanthe sat up in bed and glanced at her alarm clock. It had only just gone six, and outside it was still pitch-black and pouring with rain.

She lay back against her pillow. Who cared what the weather was doing? She was thirteen – a teenager at last – and that was all that mattered. She had finally caught up with Grace, whose birthday was in September. Now the pair of them could be teenagers together.

Not that it felt any different being thirteen. She was excited, of course – it was impossible not to be, especially with the party to look forward to at the weekend – but she'd expected to wake up feeling changed in some way: not just the same old Xanthe Fox she'd always been.

Her heart lurched at the thought of Saturday night's party. She reckoned Saul might ask her to dance, but she wasn't sure. He was certainly taking more notice of her these days. Ever since the summer holidays, when she and Grace had bumped into him down in the park and they'd spent the afternoon messing about on the boating lake together, he'd seemed more attentive towards her. But that didn't necessarily mean he felt the same way about her as she did about him. She really mustn't get her hopes up.

She fought back the butterflies that were rising from the pit of her stomach.

Mum and Dad would be in at seven with an armful of presents and cards, and Mum would be bound to get all soppy and sentimental, like she always did on her birthday. She'd open one or two of the presents and save the rest till after her birthday dinner this evening.

She jumped as her mobile beeped from her bedside table. Who on earth would be texting her at this time? She picked it up and checked the screen. It was a message from Grandma Alice.

Wanted to be the first to wish U a HAPPY BIRTHDAY, it read. *Looking forward to seeing U tomorrow. GGA xx*

Xanthe grinned at her great-grandmother's

text-speak: it had taken weeks to teach her how to use that phone. She rolled on to her stomach and keyed in a reply.

Thanks! But what R U doing up at this time of the morning? Couldn't U sleep?

Her phone beeped again almost at once.

Too excited about your birthday! Such a big day for U. Such a big day for us ALL!

Xanthe smiled. That was a bit over the top! It wasn't as if Grandma Alice was even coming to the birthday dinner tonight.

She put her mobile back on the bedside table and pulled the duvet up over her head. It wasn't long before she had drifted off into a strange sort of half-sleep, where images of a paint-splattered Miss Evans gave way to pictures of her great-grandmother, propped up in bed in her pink fleecy dressing gown and tapping away on her mobile.

She was awoken by a knock at her bedroom door. Before she could respond, her parents came barging into the room, her mother carrying a stack of cards and presents and her father following on behind.

"Happy birthday!" exclaimed her mother, piling everything on to the bed and bending forwards to give Xanthe a kiss. "Look at all these presents! I expect you'll want to wait till later to unwrap most of them, but there's one from us I thought you could open now."

Xanthe's father drew back the curtains on to the gloomy morning, then sat down on the end of the bed and grinned. "Many happy returns, sweetheart! Hope it's a great one!"

Mrs Fox shook her head in disbelief. "Thirteen years old!" she said, settling herself next to her husband. "And it still seems like only yesterday you were born! Such a storm there was in the middle of the night. I remember getting to the hospital just as dawn was breaking."

Xanthe rolled her eyes.

"Here we go again," murmured her father. "Brace yourself, Xanthe!"

"The rain was clearing and the sun was just coming up," went on Mrs Fox. "A beautiful ball of red over the horizon." She sniffed. "I couldn't help feeling it meant something, somehow."

Xanthe began slitting open her birthday cards and passing them over to her father to read.

"Such a funny screwed-up face you had. Such a squashy little nose and—"

"*Sally!*" interrupted Mr Fox. "Give the girl a break, for goodness' sake."

His wife dabbed her eyes with the corner of her

dressing gown and laughed. "All right! All right! I'm sorry, I just can't seem to help myself!" She handed Xanthe a rectangular parcel, wrapped in pale pink paper. "Here you are. This is the one we wanted you to open before school."

Xanthe tore off the wrapping paper. Inside was a gold notebook, its covers held together by a tiny lock.

"I thought you could use it as a diary," said her mother. "Feelings can get a bit complicated at your age – and writing things down helps, I promise."

Xanthe unlocked the notebook and leafed through the creamy white sheets. "It's gorgeous." She leaned forwards and gave her mother a hug. "Thank you, both of you. I love it." She put it down on her bedside table. "There's just one other present I want to open now," she said, sifting through the pile on her bed. "The one from Grandma Alice. She said she gave it to you, Mum."

Mrs Fox nodded. She picked out a small, tissue-wrapped package and passed it to Xanthe. "This is the one. She was most particular about it. Wouldn't let me go till I'd zipped it up in the inside pocket of my handbag."

Xanthe unwrapped the package carefully. "Oh!" she exclaimed. "It's her locket! I *thought* there was something different about her yesterday." She held up the battered little oval of silver by its chain and cast her eyes over it. On the back she could just make out the faded shape of a letter E engraved into the casing, something she'd not seen when it had hung round her great-grandmother's neck. "What d'you think that stands for?" she asked, holding the locket out to her mother.

Mrs Fox shook her head. "I've no idea. I've never seen it close up before. Goodness me, Xanthe. You really must be very special to your Grandma Alice. I don't think I've ever seen her without her locket."

Prising it open, Xanthe drew out a piece of paper and unfolded it. Tears pricked her eyes as she read out the message written in her great-grandmother's looping hand: "A very special present for a very special great-granddaughter."

"She knows how much I love it," she said, her voice catching.

Mr Fox glanced down at the locket. "What are you going to put inside it?"

Xanthe thought for a moment. "I'm not sure. When I saw Grandma Alice yesterday she said my present was in two halves, and that she'd give me the second part when I went round for tea tomorrow, so I can't help thinking it might be a photo to go inside. That's what *she* kept in it: a photo of her and Great-Granddad Bill, taken on their wedding day."

Mr Fox glanced at his watch. "Goodness!" he exclaimed, jumping to his feet. "Look at the time. We'd better get a move on." He leaned over and ruffled Xanthe's hair. "We'll continue with the celebrations tonight."

Mrs Fox got up and followed her husband out of the room. "I'll go and sort out some breakfast," she called over her shoulder. "Don't be too long, birthday girl."

Xanthe swung her legs out of bed and scooped up her clothes on her way to the bathroom.

She was nearly at the door when she turned and went back for the locket.

It was against school rules to wear jewellery. No bracelets. No fancy hairslides. No earrings other than the simplest of studs. But no one was going to notice if she wore the locket under her shirt, were they? It would be nice to feel she had Grandma Alice close to her today.

It might even bring her luck.

Xanthe grinned with delight as her classmates gathered round in the playground to wish her happy birthday. She couldn't believe how many cards she'd got. Apart from Kelly, the only person in her class who hadn't come up to her was Donna, but that wasn't very surprising considering they hardly knew each other. Saul had even given her a birthday hug, which had started the butterflies off in her stomach again.

The bell rang and everyone began to drift towards the main entrance.

"Wow!" said Grace, taking Xanthe's arm. "What a lot of cards! Aren't you the popular one!" She gave Donna a cheery smile as they passed her. "You don't mind waiting till Saturday for your present, do you? We had to order it off the internet and it hasn't come yet."

"Of course I don't mind," said Xanthe. She pulled a face. "Mind you, I wish it *was* the weekend right now. After what happened yesterday, I feel a bit nervous about school today."

Grace squeezed her arm. "Everything'll be fine, I'm sure. No one's said a word about it, have they? And I bet most people suspect Kelly anyway."

"Yeah, but what if she tries something else? What if she's really got it in for me this term?"

"She's hardly going to do anything today, is she?" said Grace. "Not two days running. She wouldn't have the nerve." They made their way into school and headed towards their classroom. "Did you tell your mum and dad what happened?"

Xanthe shook her head. "I didn't want to upset

36

them. Don't say anything when you come round tonight, will you?"

"Of course I won't."

"I told Grandma Alice, though," said Xanthe. "I didn't mean to, but she kind of wheedled it out of me."

She glanced over her shoulder, then pulled out the little silver locket from beneath her shirt. "This is what she gave me for my birthday. It used to belong to her and now she's passed it on to me. Isn't it beautiful?"

Grace looked down at the locket. "Oh, Xanthe!" she breathed. "It's gorgeous." She frowned. "You'd better not let anyone see it, though. If Mr Maguire catches you wearing it, he'll go mental."

Xanthe nodded. "I know. Don't worry. I'll be careful."

Mr Wood came down the corridor towards them, and she tucked the locket hurriedly back inside her shirt.

Today was going to be a whole new start. Nobody was going to spoil her birthday.

Not even Kelly Snier.

4.
The Maths Test

Miss Pimm surveyed the class over the rim of her tortoiseshell glasses. "You'll be pleased to hear we're going to spend most of this lesson covering a new topic. It's high time you were introduced to the delights of Pythagoras' theorem."

Xanthe groaned to herself. Pythagoras' theorem? What on earth was that? It sounded terrible. Like a disease or something.

"However," went on Miss Pimm, "I thought we'd start with a short test to get those maths brains of yours working again after the Christmas break."

Xanthe's heart sank even further. A test? On their second day back? What a way to spend her thirteenth birthday. She exchanged glances with Grace, who was sitting beside her.

"It'll help me find out what you've remembered from last term," said Miss Pimm. "See if there are any areas we need to revisit." She began to walk round the classroom, handing out sheets of paper. "Please don't turn over your tests until I tell you to."

Xanthe eyed the sheet in front of her. Knowing Miss Pimm, it would be completely impossible.

The teacher returned to her desk and checked her watch. "You have fifteen minutes to complete the test. Don't forget to write your name on your sheet. You may begin."

Xanthe turned over her paper. She scribbled her name at the top and looked at the first question.

Long multiplication! All that carrying and remembering to put the noughts in the right places. If she tried to do this one first she'd panic and mess the whole test up for sure. Better to leave it out and go back to it later on.

The next few questions were on shapes and graphs. As long as she took things nice and slowly she'd probably be OK with these. They looked more like art than maths, really. A collection of drawings with a few numbers thrown in for good measure.

A couple of tables along from her, she could see Kelly scribbling away furiously. Kelly was amazing at maths. You could practically hear her brain whirring as she worked. She had probably done the long multiplication question in seconds.

Xanthe completed the questions on shapes and graphs and glanced through the rest of the paper, which was all on fractions.

She was *terrible* at fractions. When it came to numerators and denominators her brain just seemed to shut down.

She pressed her fingers against her forehead. She could feel a headache coming on, a dull thumping sensation that was worsening by the minute. Leaving the fractions questions blank, she went back to the long multiplication at the top of the page.

Six nines were fifty-four, weren't they? Put down the four. Carry the five. Four fours were sixteen…

A commotion nearby made her glance up. Donna had dropped her pencil case, and everyone was staring at the scattered collection of pens and pencils on the floor: everyone, that was, except Kelly, who had obviously finished her test already and was sitting back in her seat looking at Xanthe, the corners of her mouth twisted into a sarcastic smile.

"Keep going, everyone!" instructed Miss Pimm. "You've only got half a minute left. I'll pick up your things, Donna."

Forcing herself to ignore Kelly's gaze, Xanthe returned her attention to the question. Nine sevens … she hated this one. She started to go through her nine times table, but her head was pounding now, and the numbers seemed to be blurring before her eyes. Nine sevens … nine sevens…

She blinked, then stared again at the test paper.

The multiplication sign was glowing bright red.

"Time's up!" announced Miss Pimm. "Turn over your sheets and put your pens down."

Xanthe turned her test paper over. She squeezed her eyes shut, then opened them wide. Had she imagined that glowing shape? Was her mind playing tricks on her? Certainly her head was throbbing fit to burst.

"Right, settle down, please," said Miss Pimm. "I'll write up the answers and you can mark each other's tests." She redistributed the papers before making her way up to the whiteboard. "I'll check the results myself later on."

Xanthe glanced at the sheet in front of her. It belonged to Alex Macpherson, Saul's best friend, and it looked like he'd managed to answer all of the questions, including the long multiplication one. She ferreted around in her pencil case for a different coloured pen. Her head still ached, but at least her vision had gone back to normal: the multiplication sign on Alex's paper definitely wasn't glowing.

"Miss Pimm?"

Miss Pimm turned round. "Yes? What is it, Kelly?"

Kelly scraped back her chair and got to her feet, brandishing the test paper she had been given. "You'd better see," she said, marching up to the front.

Silence fell around the room as Miss Pimm scanned the piece of paper. Her face turned an unpleasant shade of purple.

"Thank you, Kelly," she said. "You may go back to your seat." She cleared her throat. "Xanthe. Come here, please. It would seem you have some explaining to do."

Xanthe frowned. She couldn't be in trouble already, surely? Miss Pimm hadn't even written the answers on the board yet.

She shot a quick glance at Grace, then walked up to the front of the classroom.

"I suppose you think you're being funny?" snapped Miss Pimm, thrusting the sheet of paper at her.

Xanthe stared down at the test paper and gasped. A thick line had been slashed across it, and at the bottom, in her own handwriting, were the words, *Miss Pimm's maths class stinks.*

"But…" she began.

"But what? Are you telling me this isn't your paper?"

Xanthe's eyes flitted over the sheet. There was her

name at the top, and beneath the slash she could see the unfinished long multiplication question, the completed middle section, and all those fractions at the end left blank.

"Well?"

"It — it *is* my paper. But I didn't put that line through it. Or write that at the bottom. It wasn't me, really it wasn't…"

"Things like this don't just happen by accident," said Miss Pimm. "This is your handwriting, isn't it?"

Xanthe bit her lip. Out of the corner of her eye she could see Kelly sitting with her head bent, her shoulders shaking with silent laughter.

"Yes," she murmured. "It is. But I didn't do it, Miss Pimm. Really I didn't. It must've been—"

Miss Pimm held up her hand to silence her.

"I don't want to hear any excuses, thank you."

She tore a sheet of paper from a notebook on her desk and began to write.

"Take this to Mr Maguire," she commanded. She sealed the note and test paper in an envelope and thrust it into Xanthe's hand. "Let's see what he has to say."

Xanthe's eyes filled with tears.

She blundered towards the door, her gaze sweeping the classroom.

Grace was leaning forwards in her chair, her face

full of support and concern – but in Saul's eyes there was an altogether different look, a look that told her all she needed to know.

That he was no longer sure what to believe.

Xanthe hovered outside Mr Maguire's office, her heart racing.

She'd been there nearly five minutes now, and with every passing second her courage was fading. Each time she raised her hand to knock on the door she lowered it again, terrified of what the headmaster was going to say. She was almost certainly about to get her first ever detention – and on her birthday, too.

To her left was the Honours Corridor, which ran the entire length of the school hall. It was lined with scores of wooden boards bearing the names of all the successful Milchester High students. She was sure none of them had ever found themselves standing outside the headmaster's office waiting to be punished.

She jumped as the office door swung open.

"Xanthe!" exclaimed Mr Maguire. He smiled down at her. "Have you come to see me?"

Xanthe glanced away. If she tried to speak she'd probably start crying. She held out the envelope, her hand shaking. Her head still ached so much it was making her feel sick.

Mr Maguire opened the envelope and scanned its contents. His smile faded. "You'd better come in," he said, standing back to let Xanthe past. "I must say, you're one of the last people I might have expected to land themselves in trouble."

He motioned for her to take a seat at his desk and sat down opposite her. "Why, the last time you were in here you signed the Book of Excellence, didn't you?"

Xanthe nodded, watching as the headmaster picked up a red book from the side of the desk and began leafing through its pages.

"Here we are," he said. *"Xanthe Fox. For generosity of spirit and exceptional manners."* He leaned back in his chair and folded his arms. "So what's gone wrong? Your behaviour in maths sounds completely out of character."

"I didn't do it," began Xanthe. "Honestly, I didn't."

"Then who did?"

Xanthe hesitated.

"I – I think it might've been Kelly Snier," she said at last. "I don't want to tell tales or anything, but she was the one who got my paper to mark and—"

"Miss Pimm tells me in her note that the remark at the bottom of the test is in your handwriting," interrupted the headmaster. "And that she had only just given out the papers when Kelly drew her attention to it. She wouldn't have had time to copy your writing in such a short space of time. Assuming she'd wanted to in the first place." He frowned. "Do you two girls not get on?"

Xanthe said nothing.

"Let me put it another way," went on Mr Maguire. "Has Kelly ever done anything like this in the past?"

Again, Xanthe hesitated. If she told the headmaster what had happened in art yesterday, she might find herself in an even worse mess than the one she was in already. Slowly, she shook her head.

"In which case, I would strongly suggest you take your own advice and cut the tale-telling," advised the headmaster.

Xanthe glared down at the carpet, silently tracing its pattern of blue and red triangles. Under the collar of her shirt she could feel the cool silver of Grandma Alice's locket against her skin. So much for bringing her good luck.

"Is there something worrying you, Xanthe? Are there any problems I should know about? At school? Or at home, maybe?"

Xanthe bit her lip. If he'd asked her that two days ago, she'd have said no, but now her life was starting to look like one big problem. She was in trouble at school and it looked as if the boy she liked thought she was a liar. To top it all, she had a splitting headache and she seemed to be seeing things. Or at least she had in maths. That glowing red shape on her test paper had been seriously freaky.

"Well, if you're not going to talk to me, I'm afraid I've no option but to give you a lunchtime detention," said Mr Maguire. "Now, off you go: the bell's about to ring for break. I don't want to see you in here again all term, Xanthe. Not unless it's to sign the Book of Excellence. Understood?"

Xanthe nodded. She stumbled to her feet and made for the door.

At the other end of the corridor she could see her class streaming out of maths. Saul was walking next to Donna, who was smiling at him and nodding enthusiastically at something he was saying.

She watched as the pair of them disappeared through the double doors, swallowing back a sob that threatened to erupt from deep inside her.

Right now she couldn't remember ever feeling so miserable.

5.
Birthday Dinner

"*Please* cheer up," said Grace, following Xanthe down the path and waiting while her friend rummaged around in her bag for her keys. "I know you've had a terrible day, but you've got to forget about it now. You mustn't let Kelly get to you like this."

Xanthe slid her key into the lock and pushed open the front door. "It's not just Kelly who's upsetting me," she said. "It's Saul, too. He's hardly said a word to me since maths. And he's been giving me these weird looks, as if he doesn't know what to think."

She led the way inside. "We've been getting on so well, and I thought he really liked me, so why didn't he stick up for me today? Why didn't he believe me when I told him it had to be another of Kelly's nasty tricks?"

Grace put down her school bag and took off her coat. "I'm sure he *wants* to believe you, Xanthe. I expect he just can't see how Kelly managed to copy your handwriting so quickly."

"Oh, so now *you* don't believe me?"

"I didn't *say* that. Of course I believe you. I was just pointing out that Kelly acted pretty fast, that's all."

Xanthe slumped down on the bottom step of the stairs. "Sorry," she said. "I didn't mean to snap at you. *I* don't really understand how she managed to do it, either." She buried her face in her hands. "Ignore me. I've had this awful headache all day and everything's getting on top of me. *Everything.* I know this sounds ridiculous, but when I came out of Mr Maguire's office this morning I saw Saul talking to Donna and it made me feel really left out."

Grace gawped at her. "Yes, that *does* sound ridiculous. You know Saul. He was probably just trying to include her in things and make her feel welcome. You should try doing the same – she seems really nice." She sighed. "Come on, Xanthe! You're bigger than this. If you're not careful you're going to end up as warped as Kelly. Don't forget, she's the one causing all the trouble. She'll still be smarting after what Saul said yesterday – and I shouldn't think you having a party and inviting nearly everyone except her is helping matters, either. Things'll calm down after the weekend, I bet."

She held out her hands and pulled Xanthe to her feet. "Let's go up to your room and chill out before your mum and dad get home. I've got something important I want to talk to you about."

"Like what?" asked Xanthe suspiciously.

Grace looked back at her friend, her face solemn. "Like what we're going to wear on Saturday night, of course!" she said. "What could be more important than that?"

Grace leaned back on Xanthe's bed.

"So, that's settled, then," she said. "You're wearing your green dress, shimmery tights and boots, and I'm coming in jeans and my new top." She shook out her long black hair. "I can't wait for Saturday. It's going to be brilliant!"

"I hope so," said Xanthe. She frowned suddenly. "D'you reckon Saul's still going to come? After today, I mean?"

Grace shot her a warning look. "Don't start all that again. I'm sure he'll be there." She stretched her leg across the bed and nudged Xanthe with her foot. "Now, are you going to show me what you got for your birthday? I'm dying to see."

Xanthe managed a small laugh. "You know I've

got to wait till this evening before I open my presents. That way Mum and Dad get to string out the celebrations as long as they can. I guess it's the price I pay for being an only child."

"You don't know how lucky you are!" replied Grace. "I'd swap my brothers for being an only child any day." She glanced round Xanthe's room. "So haven't you opened *anything*? Not even one little present?"

"Only Grandma Alice's," said Xanthe. "But you've seen that already." Her hand went up to the locket round her neck. "Oh, and I got a diary from Mum and Dad."

She picked up the gold notebook from her bedside table and passed it over to Grace.

"Mum's got it into her head that now I'm thirteen I'm going to need something to confide all my complicated feelings in."

"Yeah, right! The second you turn thirteen everything changes. Just like that. You turn purple and sprout two heads."

Xanthe giggled. "It's gorgeous, all the same. And if the last two days are anything to go by, Mum might just have a point. Though I reckon it's going to take more than a diary to keep me sane right now."

Grace reached over and squeezed her hand. "Try not to think about it. Like I said, things'll get easier after the weekend, you'll see."

From her pocket, Xanthe's mobile beeped.

She took it out and scanned the message. "It's Grandma Alice. She wants to know if I'm having a good birthday."

"Are you going to tell her the truth?"

Xanthe shook her head. "No way." She started to tap in a reply. "I feel bad enough moaning on at her about what happened in art yesterday."

"But I thought you two were like best friends. I thought you told each other everything."

"Well, I'm not going to tell her about this," said Xanthe firmly. She finished off the text and put her phone back in her pocket. "Sometimes I reckon it's best just to keep quiet."

She slid off the bed as a car pulled up outside the house. "Mum's back. Come on. Let's go down and say hello."

Mr Fox leaned back in his chair and sighed.

"That was delicious!" he said, throwing down his napkin. "Three different kinds of pizza and the best tiramisu I've ever tasted!" He beamed across the table at Xanthe. "Food fit for a thirteen-year-old, I'd say!"

Xanthe smiled back at him weakly. The headache she'd had since maths was still niggling away, and she felt completely wiped out. It would be a relief when Grace had gone home and she could sneak off to her room.

"We're not finished yet," said her mother. She crossed over to the sideboard and came back carrying a huge chocolate cake with Xanthe's name written on the top. "I'm sure you can all manage a slice of this."

Grace looked at the cake and grinned. "I see you're still not risking any candles, Xanthe!"

Xanthe blushed. "Definitely not. You know what I'm like when it comes to flames, even if they *are* only tiny ones."

She sighed to herself. She'd been scared of fire ever since she could remember. There was no explanation for it – but it terrified her to the core. One of her very first memories was of a Bonfire Night party she'd been taken to by her parents when she was three or four years old. She could still recall the stench of the smoke and the loud explosions above her head as the fireworks burst into life, spraying multicoloured stars across the sky. But it wasn't the fireworks that had been the problem. What had scared the living daylights out of her was the bonfire itself, its flames leaping and curling into the darkness like dragons' tongues. She'd screamed and screamed until her parents had given up trying to console her and taken her home.

"Xanthe? Are you going to make a wish? Before you cut the cake?"

Xanthe roused herself from her thoughts. She picked up the knife that was lying beside the cake and positioned it over the icing. She didn't have to think too hard about what to wish for this year. Right now there was only one thing she wanted.

And that was for everything to go back to normal.

Xanthe pulled on her pyjamas and got into bed.

So much for turning thirteen. What with the maths test and the lunchtime detention and Saul being all distant with her, she couldn't remember ever having had such a bad day. No wonder she still had a headache.

She reached for her mobile and checked her messages. Waiting for her was another text from Grandma Alice.

Glad U R having a great day, sweetheart. Can't wait to give U the 2nd part of your present.

Xanthe allowed herself a tiny smile. At least someone was enjoying her birthday.

It can't be as brilliant as the first part, she typed back. *I love my locket SO much. What does the E stand for on the back, by the way?*

She glanced at her watch. She wouldn't be getting any more texts from her great-grandmother tonight. By now she'd be watching one of her trashy soaps on telly.

She started as less than a minute later her mobile beeped again.

Will tell U what it stands for tomorrow, read the text. *Can't wait to see U!*

Xanthe's eyes filled with tears. How good it would be to ring her great-grandmother right now and explain about Kelly's mean little trick in maths and the meeting with Mr Maguire. She could even tell her about that freaky glowing multiplication sign she'd seen – or *thought* she'd seen. She didn't want to tell anyone else about it – they'd think she was losing the plot – but Grandma Alice wouldn't make fun of her, would she?

Then again, the last thing she wanted to do was worry her. Perhaps she'd better leave it.

Xanthe switched off her mobile and huddled under the duvet. She could hear her parents murmuring to one another in the hallway below.

"She didn't seem herself this evening, Robert," her mother was saying. "There was something bugging her. D'you think Kelly's said something to upset her again?"

"Maybe," replied her father. "Or else it could be to

do with Saul. I think she's pretty keen on him."

Xanthe squirmed beneath the duvet.

She pulled it round her more closely, trying to shut out the expression she had seen on Saul's face as she'd left the classroom. He had looked as if he no longer trusted her. As if he didn't recognize her, even.

Well, who could blame him?

Right now she wasn't sure she recognized herself.

6.
Science

Xanthe got off the bus and headed towards the school gates. She had woken with another headache, and what had begun as a nagging pain in her temples had now spread to her entire forehead. She hadn't eaten any breakfast, either. Just the thought of going into school today made her stomach churn.

In spite of Grace's warning, she'd put on her locket again this morning. True, it hadn't brought her much luck yesterday, but she didn't want to be without it. In any case, she was going straight to Grandma Alice's after school, and if her hunch was correct and the second part of her present really was a photo to put inside it, then it made sense to have it with her.

She passed through the gates and glanced around the playground. It would have been good to have had a few minutes with Saul to patch things up, but it didn't look like his bus had come in yet. The only person she could see from her class was Donna.

She blushed, embarrassed at how jealous she'd felt yesterday. Who was she to mind if Saul wanted to make friends with the new girl? She could remember all too well how *she* had felt, starting at Milchester High – and she'd been with everyone from primary school. Donna had no one.

She squinted up at the January sky. Maybe she should take Grace's advice and try to get to know her, too. If she was keen on art, then at least they'd have something to talk about. She could even invite her to the party at the weekend.

She was jolted from her thoughts by the sound of someone speaking her name, and turned to see Saul standing close by.

"Saul!" she exclaimed, the colour rushing to her cheeks once more. "I didn't see your bus come in."

Saul shuffled his feet. "Dad gave me a lift this morning. I – I wanted to get in early so I could talk to you." He cleared his throat. "Look – about what happened in maths yesterday. I'm sorry if it seemed like I didn't believe you. I know there's no way you would've done a thing like that, but at the time I couldn't see *how* Kelly had managed it. She's even cleverer than I thought."

"She's very clever," agreed Xanthe, her heart lifting. She dropped her gaze. "Does – does that mean you're still coming to my party?"

"Of *course* I'm still coming. Why would you think I wouldn't be?"

"Oh, I don't know, I just … never mind." Xanthe smiled. "I thought I might ask Donna, too," she said. "Then she can get to know some of us a bit better."

"That's a great idea," said Saul. He waved at Donna across the playground. "I'm sure she'll be really pleased."

There was a moment's silence.

"Friends, then?" said Saul.

Xanthe nodded. She suddenly felt ravenously hungry and her headache had all but disappeared.

"Friends!" she grinned.

"In science this morning," announced Dr Flinders, "we're going to look at how different metals react in acid." He gestured towards a row of trays on one of the shelves behind him. "Come up and collect the samples I've put out for you. Please use a fresh test tube of dilute hydrochloric acid for each experiment, and don't forget to write down a description of the reactions."

Xanthe groaned to herself. It was going to be a very long morning. Still, at least Saul was her lab partner, as usual. There'd been an awkward moment just now, when it looked like he'd promised to be partners with Donna, but Grace had stepped in and saved the day by offering to pair up with her instead.

"I'll go and fetch the samples, shall I?" she said to Saul, watching as he set up a row of test tubes in the rack in front of them. "Then you can get on with the exciting part."

Saul pulled a face. "I can't think it's going to be very exciting," he murmured. "Dr Flinders is hardly going to let us loose with any interesting metals, is he?" He began to pour acid into the test tubes. "My brother says you have to wait till you're in the Sixth Form before you start doing any proper experiments. Apparently you get to handle chemicals that really react then, instead of ones that just fizz around for a bit or sit at the bottom of a test tube doing nothing."

Xanthe grinned. "I'll see what I can find," she said, getting up from her chair.

She made her way to the front of the lab and helped herself to a small plastic dish and a pair of tweezers.

"Behaving yourself today, are you?" whispered Kelly, who was standing nearby. "Makes a change."

Xanthe forced herself to say nothing.

She began to collect the various metals, and was about halfway along the row of trays when Kelly jogged against her, sending several of the samples to the floor.

Leaving her dish on the shelf, Xanthe bent down to pick them up, her lips pressed tightly together. She wasn't even going to look at Kelly, let alone get into an argument with her. She wouldn't give her the satisfaction. She'd just put the metals back in the dish and pretend nothing had happened.

She collected the last few samples from their trays and returned to the workbench.

"There you go," she said, handing the dish to Saul. "D'you know what any of them are?"

Saul inspected the array of metals.

"That one's copper," he said, pointing to an orangey-pink square. "I don't think there'll be much of a reaction there." He picked it up with the tweezers and dropped it into one of the test tubes, watching as it sank to the bottom. "There! What did I tell you?" He scribbled something down in his workbook, then turned back to the dish and selected a long silvery strip. "Now, this should be a bit more interesting. Magnesium ribbon. I've got some in my chemistry set at home." He added it to the next test tube.

"Brilliant!" exclaimed Xanthe as it began to fizz

and bubble in the acid. "I like that one!" She poked about in the dish. "What about this? What d'you reckon this is?"

Saul shrugged. "Not sure," he said, glancing down at the sample. "Zinc, maybe? Let's try it out."

Xanthe watched as he picked it up. Then she craned forwards. Where only a moment before she had seen nothing more interesting than a lump of greyish metal, now a strange shape was lighting up its surface – a shape just like the one she had seen in maths the previous day ... a glowing red X.

Hardly knowing what she was doing, she reached out to stop Saul from dropping the sample into the test tube – but it was too late: there was a loud bang, then a splintering sound as the test tube exploded into tiny pieces.

Screams filled the lab. Everyone leaped away from the workbench, tripping over stools and knocking them to the floor. Xanthe could see Grace and Donna in one corner, their eyes wide.

Dr Flinders was beside them in an instant. "What on *earth*...?" he started, staring at the mess in front of him. "What in heaven's name did you add to that acid?"

Saul looked back at him, pale-faced.

"I don't know what it was, sir," he said. "I-I thought it might've been a piece of zinc..."

"Zinc!" exclaimed Dr Flinders. "Zinc wouldn't react like that!"

He rounded on Xanthe.

"You came up and collected the metals, didn't you?"

Xanthe nodded.

"And you're sure you only took the samples I put out on the bottom shelf?"

"I–I'm quite sure…"

Dr Flinders turned to Saul.

"And you poured the acid into the test tubes?"

"Yes, sir…"

"You used the acid I put out on the workbenches? The dilute hydrochloric?"

"Yes, sir. Of course, sir…"

There was a long silence.

"I can only conclude," said Dr Flinders at last, "that one of you is not telling the truth. The most reactive metal I put out in those trays was magnesium, and that wouldn't have reacted anything like as strongly as this." He glanced down at the shards of broken glass. "Either something went into that acid that shouldn't have done, or else you've been into one of the back cupboards and got hold of a different strength of acid. Either way, what you have done is quite extraordinarily dangerous. You will both go to Mr Maguire and explain yourselves immediately."

Xanthe bowed her head. She followed Saul out of the lab, her cheeks burning.

"Great," muttered Saul when the door had closed behind them and they were heading towards Mr Maguire's office. "Thanks a lot for dragging me down with you."

Xanthe reached out and grabbed him by the arm. "What d'you mean?" she said fiercely. "It wasn't anything to do with *me*."

Saul pulled away.

"Well, it wasn't anything to do with *me*! Oh, come on, Xanthe. We both know it was you. You nicked something off the top shelf to make things a bit more interesting, didn't you? Because of what I said about the experiments my brother's allowed to do in the Sixth Form. You did it to get on the right side of me after what happened yesterday."

Xanthe gaped at him.

"Don't be stupid!" she exclaimed. "Do you really think I'd risk something like this just to impress you? After all the trouble I've been in?" She stopped in the middle of the corridor and turned to face him. "Listen to me a minute, will you? When I was up at the front getting the samples, Kelly nudged me and made me drop some of them. I bet you she added something to my dish while I was picking them up."

Saul shook his head at her and sighed. "It's always

64

Kelly's fault, isn't it? Every single time something goes wrong you blame it on her."

"No, I don't…"

"Yes, you do…"

There was a pause.

"Did – did you notice anything weird?" asked Xanthe. "About the metal, I mean?"

"Weird? What sort of weird?"

"I – I thought I saw something strange on it. Something—"

Xanthe broke off. She couldn't bring herself to mention the glowing X shape. Saul was already staring at her as if he no longer believed a word she said.

"I don't know what to make of you right now, Xanthe," he said. "I don't know what's got into you." He put his hands in his pockets and stalked off down the corridor in front of her. "You've turned into a first-class trouble magnet."

The journey from Mr Maguire's office back to the classroom had never seemed so long. Break had just started and Xanthe had to keep her head bent to avoid the stares of passing students. She was obviously gaining quite a reputation. Saul had already stormed off outside, muttering something about getting as far away from her as possible.

It had been terrible back there in the office – much worse than it had been the day before. Mr Maguire had grilled them both about what had happened, and when they hadn't come up with any satisfactory answers, he'd given them a massive lecture about irresponsible behaviour and put them on lunchtime detention. After what Saul had said to her in the corridor, she'd decided not to mention her suspicions about Kelly to the headmaster: she didn't want to be accused of being a telltale again.

Grace was waiting for her outside the classroom. "Come on," she murmured, taking her arm. "Let's go and find somewhere quiet."

Xanthe nodded, not trusting herself to speak. She followed Grace up the stairs towards the lockers, then on into the library.

"Well?" said Grace when they were sitting together in a deserted corner. "What did he say?"

Xanthe shrugged. "He gave us a detention and told us he'd contact our parents if there was any more trouble." Her eyes brimmed with tears. "Honestly, Grace, I don't know what's going on. It's as if my life isn't my own any more."

There was a long silence.

"So what exactly *did* happen in science?" asked Grace at last.

Xanthe sighed. "I'm not sure. All I can tell you is

that when I went up to get the samples, Kelly elbowed me and made me drop some of them on the floor. The only explanation I can think of is that she took something off the top shelf and put it in my dish when I wasn't looking."

"And did you try telling that to Mr Maguire?"

Xanthe shook her head. "I've got no *proof* it was Kelly, have I? And anyway, after yesterday, when Mr Maguire accused me of telling tales, I thought I should just keep quiet."

"What does Saul think happened?"

"He reckons it was me who did it. That I wanted to get in his good books by spicing things up a bit. As *if*!"

The bell rang to signal the start of lessons, and Grace got to her feet.

"Wait," said Xanthe, pulling her friend back down beside her. "There's – there's something else. Something I need to tell you before we go."

Grace glanced at her watch. "Can't it wait till later? I've got to get my stuff out of my locker before French. And don't you have a piano lesson to get to?"

"It won't take long," said Xanthe. She stared down at her hands. "And besides, if I don't tell you now, I might not feel like it later on."

"What d'you mean?"

"I can trust you, can't I?"

"Of course you can. Oh, Xanthe, you've got me worried. What on earth's the matter?"

Xanthe took a deep breath. "Just before Saul dropped that bit of metal into the test tube," she said, "I – I saw something strange."

"Something strange? Like what exactly?"

Xanthe paused. "A sort of glowing shape on the surface of the metal. A luminous red X."

Grace's eyes widened.

"It was the same in maths yesterday," went on Xanthe. "You know, when we were doing the test. I was trying to answer the first question, and just before Miss Pimm told us to stop and turn over our sheets, the multiplication sign began to glow. It happened so quickly, I wasn't completely sure I'd seen it. But this time I definitely did. Something seriously weird's going on, Grace – and I seem to be at the centre of it all. It's really beginning to freak me out—" She broke off. "You don't believe me, do you?"

For a moment Grace didn't reply.

"What about in art?" she said finally. "You know, when the paint went all over Miss Evans. Did you see this – er – glowing shape then, too?"

Xanthe frowned, trying to recall the precise moment the paint had arched up into the air.

"No," she said. "I don't think I did. But I did today. I wasn't imagining it, really I wasn't." She shot her friend a pleading glance.

Grace sighed. "Look, Xanthe. You're my best mate, right?"

"Right…"

"And if you want my advice – well, I think you should tell your parents about this and get them to take you to the doctor's."

"Oh, so you think I'm crazy?"

"Of course I don't," said Grace gently. "But I do think it's possible there's something physically the matter with you. You had a headache the other day, didn't you? And now you're seeing strange shapes. You might need your eyes testing. That would explain things, wouldn't it?"

Xanthe considered for a moment.

It was true. She'd had a lot of headaches recently – in fact, she had one right now – but she'd put them down to the stress of the last few days. What if Grace was right? What if there was something wrong with her eyes and the answer to the weird glowing shapes lay in a simple pair of glasses? OK, they wouldn't fix everything. They certainly wouldn't fix Kelly Snier. But at least they might stop her thinking she was going out of her mind.

She looked at Grace.

"Maybe I will say something to Mum and Dad – I haven't had my eyes tested in ages. I'll leave it till after the weekend, though. I don't want to stress them out before the party."

"Good idea," said Grace. She stood up. "Come on. We're going to be late."

They made their way out of the library and headed for the lockers.

"You won't tell anyone about this, will you?" said Xanthe.

"Cross my heart."

"Especially not Saul?"

"Especially not Saul."

"He probably wouldn't be interested anyway," muttered Xanthe. "I don't think he wants anything more to do with me. He *definitely* won't be coming to my party now." She turned to Grace. "I'm going to ask Donna, by the way."

"That's a nice idea," said Grace. She frowned. "Though let's hope Kelly doesn't find out. If she discovers you've invited every girl in the class except her, it might make things even worse than they already are."

"It might indeed," said a voice in front of them. Kelly was standing at the top of the stairs, half hidden by a row of lockers. "You definitely don't want to get on the wrong side of me, Xanthe."

She clicked her tongue. "Two visits to the headmaster in as many days! One more and he'll get your parents involved. You really should be more careful."

"Ignore her," murmured Grace. "Don't let her wind you up. Get off to your piano lesson and I'll see you later."

Xanthe took her music case out of her locker and set off down the stairs.

"Poor old Xanthe," called Kelly after her. "Life's suddenly got a bit tough, hasn't it?" She gave a shrill laugh. "And something tells me it's about to get a whole lot tougher."

7.
The Fire Alarm

Xanthe closed the door to the music room.

That had been the worst piano lesson ever. She'd made mistakes in all her pieces and messed up her scales, too. No wonder Miss James had sent her away early.

She reached the top of the stairs leading out of the music wing and turned right towards the dining hall, then stopped short as a piercing wail filled her ears.

Her pulse raced.

Not the fire alarm! Please, not now! Not when Grace wasn't here to calm her down.

Retreating footsteps sounded in the distance, but her brain scarcely registered them. She gripped her music case, her palms sticky with sweat.

It was always like this. It didn't matter how many times she told herself it was only a practice, that all they would do was file into the playground for ten minutes or so, and then file back inside again, the sound of the alarm always chilled her to the bone.

She gave herself a shake.

What was she doing just standing here? She needed to get out. Everyone else in the school would be streaming into the playground by now and lining up in their forms.

At the sound of approaching sirens, her skin prickled against her clothes. What if this wasn't a fire drill, after all? What if it was for real and the building was about to fill up with fire and smoke, leaving her trapped and alone?

Tightening her grip on her music case, she began to run...

"What took you so long?" exclaimed Grace as Xanthe came hurrying across the playground to join her class. "We've been out here ages."

Xanthe slipped into line beside her friend. She stood there for a moment, unable to speak, the freezing January air stinging her face.

"I panicked," she said at last. "I was coming back from my piano lesson when the alarm went off and my mind went completely blank. I just couldn't think of the quickest way out. I ended up going past the science labs and down the computer corridor…"

"But it takes forever that way!"

"I know," said Xanthe. "I wasn't thinking straight." She gestured towards the fire engines parked in front of the school entrance. "D'you – d'you think it's for real? That there's an actual fire this time?"

Grace shook her head. "I don't think so," she said. "I can't see any flames or smoke." She leaned forwards and whispered in Xanthe's ear. "Between you and me, I reckon this might be Kelly's handiwork. She was out of the classroom at the time the alarm went off. She asked Miss Wintergreen if she could be excused and—"

She broke off as Mr Maguire strode to the front of the playground and raised his hand for silence.

"As some of you may have realized," he said, "this has not been a planned fire drill. We have reason to believe the alarm was set off as a prank."

Xanthe's eyes widened. Perhaps Grace was right. Perhaps it *was* Kelly. But why would she want to do something like that?

She glanced down the line of Year Eights. Everyone looked completely freezing, standing out here without their blazers on. Emma Hicks and Sarah Nelson were clutching each other for warmth and

Donna's pale face was even whiter than usual. A little further down stood Kelly, her blue eyes fixed on the headmaster.

"It would appear," went on Mr Maguire, "that it was an alarm near the music wing that was set off."

Xanthe stiffened. An alarm near the music wing? But that meant…

She looked more closely at Kelly. Was it her imagination, or was that the faintest of smiles on her lips?

"Rest assured, I will leave no stone unturned in finding out who is responsible," the headmaster continued. "This kind of unnecessary disruption wastes everybody's time, not least that of our emergency services. Now, please return to your classrooms in an orderly manner."

Everyone splintered from their lines and began to troop back across the playground. Saul walked past with Alex, raising his eyebrows at Xanthe as he went.

"Did you see that?" demanded Xanthe, grabbing Grace's arm. "He thinks I did it. Kelly's done it again, hasn't she? She's set me up!"

Grace frowned. "But surely she wouldn't have had time to make it as far as the music wing? She can't have been out of the classroom more than half a minute before the alarm went off."

"She could have done it if she'd really legged it. I heard footsteps, Grace. Just after the alarm started. I didn't think much about them then, but who else would it have been?"

Grace stared at her friend in silence.

"What d'you reckon I should do?" went on Xanthe. "Shall I tell Mr Maguire and hope he believes me this time? I'm in detention all lunchtime, but I could try and see him after school."

"I wouldn't," said Grace, leading the way into the main school building. "You'll only make things worse. Like you said about the other things that've happened, you've got no proof, have you? Besides, you can't go and see him after school today. We've got hockey trials, remember?"

Xanthe clapped her hand over her mouth. "Oh no! I'd completely forgotten! I'm supposed to be having tea at Grandma Alice's. There's another part to my present and she wants to give it to me. I'd better ring her."

Grace frowned. "You're not wearing your locket today, are you?"

Xanthe nodded, blushing.

"Well, where are you going to put it while we're playing hockey? You can't wear it on the pitch. And you can't just leave it in your bag. It's too precious, surely?"

"You're right," replied Xanthe as they neared their classroom. "Oh, Grace, I can't believe I've been so stupid." She lowered her voice. "I guess I'll have to hide it in my locker. It'll have to stay there overnight, though. By the time the trials have finished, the main building will be locked up."

"Whispering again, you two?" said Kelly, coming up behind them. She shook her head. "I don't know! Anyone'd think you were up to no good."

Grace rounded on her. "It was you who set off the fire alarm, wasn't it?" she hissed. "You did it to get Xanthe into even more trouble."

Kelly shrugged. "It might've been. Then again, it might not."

Grace narrowed her eyes. "What sort of a person *are* you, Kelly Snier?"

"A more interesting one than you are, clearly," Kelly spat back. She tossed her head towards Xanthe. "At least I don't hang out with *her*."

And she sauntered into the classroom, whistling softly as she went.

Xanthe hurried up the stairs towards the lockers. It had been a truly terrible day. As if the science lesson and the fire alarm hadn't been enough of an ordeal, she'd then had to suffer a whole hour of detention with Saul, who had refused to look at her the entire time. How she'd managed to get through the rest of the day she had no idea.

She took off her locket and pushed it into the back of her locker.

If only she didn't have to hide it here overnight. If only she'd remembered about the hockey trials and left it at home. Still, there was nothing to be done – this was the best place for it.

Slamming the locker door shut, she picked up her bag and headed outside to the gym.

Poor Grandma Alice. She'd sounded so disappointed when she'd rung to say she couldn't make it this afternoon. Her great-grandmother had even tried to persuade her to come along later, when the trials were over – but she'd had to say no. Her homework was already piling up and she didn't dare risk getting into even more trouble.

Xanthe glanced towards the hockey pitch. It looked like the trials were already well underway. The Year Sevens had had their turn, and Miss Hope was about to start assessing the Year Eights and Nines. Loads of students had turned up to support their friends, and there were even some parents there, too, huddled against the cold.

She reached the gym and pushed open the door to the girls' changing room.

The far end was crawling with Year Sevens getting dressed, but the rest of the room was almost deserted. There were a couple of Year Nine girls chatting beside the water fountain, but apart from them, Xanthe could only see Grace, sitting by herself on one of the benches, leaning against the racks laden with bags and blazers and hockey sticks.

"Success?" asked Grace in a low voice as Xanthe approached. "Did you manage to hide your locket?"

Xanthe nodded. "All safe in the back of my locker." She took off her blazer and hung it on a peg. "When are we on?"

Grace glanced at her watch. "About five minutes. You'd better get a move on."

Xanthe sighed. "To be honest, this is the last thing I feel like doing. After the day I've had, all I want to do is go home and hide under the duvet."

Grace fumbled inside her bag for a hairbrush. "Come on, Xanthe, you love hockey. It'll do you good. Now hurry up and get ready." She began pulling back her hair into a ponytail. "Did I tell you Mum's booked me an appointment at the hairdresser's on Saturday? I'm having it done especially for your party. I might even wear it up."

Xanthe unzipped her bag and pulled out her P.E. kit. "You'll look great however you wear it," she said, starting to get changed. "I wish I could do something interesting with *my* hair."

"You *could*, if only you'd get over your stupid hang-up about your birthmark. Honestly, Xanthe, it's so small I seriously doubt anyone would see it if you grew your hair and wore it up – and if they did, they'd probably think it was cool. I know *I* did when you first showed it to me."

Xanthe rolled her eyes. "My horrible cousin didn't think so. He thought it was hilarious. He kept saying, 'X marks the spot, X marks the spot! Xanthe's got a birthmark in the shape of an X!'" She finished getting changed and grabbed her hockey stick. "I bet you anything you like Kelly would notice it right away. That girl's got eyes like a hawk. And then I'd never hear the end of it."

A noise nearby made them start. Parting the P.E. bags hanging from the racks, they saw Donna on the other side of the bench, reaching to pick up her hockey stick from the floor.

"Donna!" exclaimed Grace. "Have you been here all this time?" She peered at the new girl more closely. "Hey, are you OK? You look terrible!"

Donna sat back down on the bench. "Actually I'm not feeling too good," she murmured. "I–I feel all strange and dizzy."

Xanthe and Grace went round to sit beside her.

"You weren't looking very well earlier on," said

Xanthe. "I couldn't help noticing how pale you were when we were outside after the fire alarm went off."

She made to put her arm round Donna's shoulders, but the new girl shrank away.

"I'll be all right," she said. "Once I get on to the hockey pitch I'll be fine." She tried to stand up, steadying herself against the bags.

"I think you should go home," said Grace. "Don't worry about the trials. I expect you'll be given another chance next week."

Donna ran her hand across her forehead. "Maybe it would be better if I left it for now." She pulled her bag towards her. "Could you tell Miss Hope for me?"

Grace nodded. "No problem. We'll go and find her right away." She reached through the bags for her hockey stick and made her way with Xanthe towards the door. "Hope you're feeling better soon."

"Poor Donna," said Xanthe when they were outside and heading for the pitch. "I hope it's nothing nasty." She swiped at a stone with her hockey stick. "You know what, Grace? If I get picked for the team, it'll be the first good thing to happen to me all week. Honestly, I'm beginning to think I might be cursed."

Grace laughed. "Oh, come on," she said. "It's not that bad. Anyway, Kelly's not doing the trials. With her out of the picture, I reckon you've got a fair chance of things going right."

Xanthe's expression brightened. "I hadn't thought of that."

They approached the pitch and her face fell.

"You spoke too soon," she muttered. She pointed to where Kelly stood amongst the other Year Eight supporters. "She might not be doing the trials, but she's turned up to watch all the same. I bet she's come to put me off."

"Well, don't let her," said Grace. "You've got to think positive, Xanthe. At this rate you're going to mess everything up before you even start playing."

Xanthe tightened her grip on her hockey stick. "You're right," she said. "I mustn't let her spoil my chances." She took a deep breath and strode towards the pitch. "I'm getting on that team whether Kelly Snier likes it or not."

8.
Revenge

Xanthe leaped off the bus and sprinted towards the school gates.

It wasn't even nine o'clock and already things weren't going well. First of all, her alarm clock hadn't gone off, and then the second bus had turned up late. She was practically the last person in, and just when she'd been hoping to get into school early to retrieve her locket.

She'd feel a whole lot happier once it was back round her neck. It might not be much use as a good luck charm, but it made her feel protected somehow. Even so, she wouldn't be bringing it into school after today. It simply wasn't worth the risk.

She ran across the playground. It was going to be another bad day, she just knew it. She would almost certainly be dragged into Mr Maguire's office and quizzed about the fire alarm – and if she ended up in any more trouble he'd be sure to contact her parents. What they'd say if they found out about everything, she couldn't begin to imagine.

The only thing keeping her going right now was the memory of yesterday's hockey trials. They'd gone like a dream. She'd handled every pass and shot as if she had planned each one in advance, and Kelly hadn't shouted out to distract her once. At least, if she had, she hadn't heard her. In fact when she'd glanced round at the crowd on her way off the pitch she hadn't even seen her. Most likely she'd stormed off in a huff, unable to stand the sight of her arch-enemy doing something right for a change.

It hadn't taken long for the bubble to burst, though. By the time she'd got home that evening she had another splitting headache and had snapped at Mum within minutes of stepping through the door. The memories of her awful day had come flooding back, and try as she might, she couldn't get away from the horrible truth: she was in deep trouble at school – and to cap it all, Saul thought she was seriously bad news.

Xanthe hurried in through the main entrance and headed for the stairs, almost colliding with Donna in her haste to get to the lockers.

"Hi," she said, pausing for a moment. "Feeling better?"

Donna blushed. "I'm fine, thanks."

Xanthe nodded. "That's good." She hesitated. "I – I've been meaning to ask whether you'd like to come to my birthday party on Saturday. I'm having a disco in town."

Donna stared at her. "You're asking me to your party?"

Xanthe smiled. "Yes. I thought it might give you the chance to get to know some of us outside school."

Donna said nothing.

"Er – well, think about it," said Xanthe into the silence. "No problem if you can't make it. I'll catch you later."

She carried on towards the lockers. That hadn't exactly gone to plan. She'd expected Donna to jump at the opportunity of coming to the party. Maybe the new girl was even shyer than they all thought.

At the top of the stairs she found her keys and opened her locker.

She reached into the back, then frowned.

She'd left the locket just behind her textbooks, hadn't she? She was sure she had...

The next minute she was emptying everything out on to the floor beside her.

It had to be in there...

Standing back, she gazed inside the locker, her blood running cold.

There was no doubt about it.

The locket had gone.

Grace gaped at Xanthe.

"You're telling me Kelly's stolen your locket?" she whispered as they filed into the hall for weekly assembly. "But *how*?"

"Maybe she sneaked off and nicked my keys out of my blazer pocket while I was doing the hockey trials," replied Xanthe fiercely. "She could've legged it over to the main building before the caretaker locked up, stolen the locket and put the keys back in my blazer before disappearing off home. It would've been dead simple." She clenched her fists. "I *wondered* why she didn't stay to give me a hard time."

They sat down beside one another.

"But how would she have known you'd put something special in your locker?" murmured Grace.

"D'you remember when we were coming back inside after the fire alarm? Just before you had a go at her about setting me up? Well, we were talking about it then. She was walking behind us, and I guess she must have heard."

Grace considered for a moment.

"So what are you going to do? Report it?"

"How can I?" muttered Xanthe. "No one's going to believe me over Kelly, are they? Not after the week I've had. In any case, I wasn't supposed to have the locket in school in the first place, and I can't afford to get into even *more* trouble." She paused. "I'll just have to get the locket back."

"And how are you going to do that exactly?"

"I'm going to have a good look around inside *her* locker."

Grace frowned. "But it might not be in there. It might be in her bag. Or she might have taken it home."

Xanthe sighed. Glancing down the line of Year Eights, she caught Saul's eye. She flushed and looked away. "I know that," she whispered. "But turning her bag inside out isn't really an option, is it? And I can hardly check out her *bedroom*. This is the only thing I can do – the only way I can fight back."

"But you can't just go snooping around in someone else's locker!"

"Why not? She's been in mine."

"You can't *prove* that…"

"No," said Xanthe. "You're right. I can't. Just like I can't prove that it was Kelly who threw the paint at Miss Evans on Monday, or that it was Kelly who landed me in trouble in maths and science, or that it

87

was Kelly who set off the fire alarm. But I know she's responsible and I'm terrified about what she might be planning next. I need that locket back, Grace. It means the world to me – and to Grandma Alice, too." She bit her lip. "Did you see that note on my desk this morning?"

Grace nodded.

"It was from Tilly Wilson, cancelling on me this Saturday. She said her mum doesn't want her getting mixed up with someone who's causing so much trouble. Can you believe it? Me, a troublemaker? And it's all because of Kelly. She's ruining my life – and somehow I've got to stop her."

There was a long silence.

"So how are you going to get hold of her key?" asked Grace at last.

"Same way she got hold of mine," said Xanthe. "I expect she keeps it in her blazer pocket. If you distract her before Spanish, I'll try and get it then. As long as I return it before break, she'll never even know it was gone."

Grace eyed her friend. "Sounds like a pretty dodgy plan to me. What if you get caught?"

"I won't," replied Xanthe. "I'll be careful, I promise."

Xanthe waited for the rest of the class to get ahead of her, then doubled-back down the corridor towards the stairs. She had three minutes at most. Three minutes to get up to the lockers, look for the locket and make it back in time for English.

So far it had gone like clockwork. As soon as they'd returned to the classroom after assembly, Grace had announced that it had started to snow and the whole class had gone rushing over to the window to look out. It had taken only a couple of seconds to slip her hand into Kelly's blazer pocket – and to her relief, the key was there. She'd then had to sit through the whole of Spanish, listening to Mr Gomez drone on and on about boring verbs, desperate to get on with the next stage of the plan.

She stole up the stairs, glancing from side to side. If anyone had told her a few days ago that she would be sneaking around school like this in between lessons, she would never have believed them. But Kelly had given her no choice.

She made straight for Kelly's locker. Sliding the key into the lock, she opened the door and looked inside.

Her heart sank. It was crammed with books and paper and half-opened packets of sweets. She'd have to take everything out to stand a chance of finding the locket.

Xanthe grabbed the nearest book and pulled it out of the locker, then reached inside for another.

"Good morning, Xanthe."

She twisted round, her heart thundering against her chest. Mr Maguire stood a short distance away, surveying her with laser-sharp eyes.

"You know you're not supposed to go back to the lockers before break," he said. "Have you forgotten something?"

"I-I was just getting a textbook for English," stammered Xanthe, her cheeks burning.

The headmaster advanced towards her.

"I see," he said. He frowned. "In which case, would you care to tell me why you are holding a geography book?"

Xanthe swallowed. "I-I…"

Mr Maguire held out his hand. "May I?"

Xanthe passed him the book in silence. She watched as he opened it and examined the name scrawled in the inside cover.

There was a long silence.

"Am I right in thinking this isn't even your locker?" said Mr Maguire at last. He stared at her, unblinking. "It seems you have some explaining to do."

9.
Blanche

"Are you telling me," said Mrs Fox, clutching her handbag to her chest, "that this is the *third* occasion my daughter has been in trouble this week?"

Mr Maguire nodded. "I'm afraid so. There was the incident beside the lockers this morning, and then the unfortunate occurrences in maths and science earlier in the week." He cleared his throat. "I also have reason to believe it may have been Xanthe who set off the fire alarm yesterday, although my investigations are ongoing."

Mrs Fox gaped at him.

"The *fire alarm…?*"

"It was set off before lunch," said the headmaster. "Xanthe was on her way back from her piano lesson, and since the alarm that was broken was one of those near the music wing, it has quite naturally been assumed—"

"Mr Maguire," interrupted Mrs Fox. "My daughter would never do a thing like that. She wouldn't be so stupid. More to the point, she's terrified of anything to do with fire. She always has been."

Xanthe shot her mother a look of gratitude before returning her attention to the pattern on the carpet. She reckoned she knew it by heart now, right down to the last blue triangle.

The headmaster raked his fingers through his hair. "Xanthe has said something similar to me herself," he said. "Though that's about all she *will* say." He shifted uncomfortably in his chair. "Anyway, as I said, I'm still carrying out my investigations. There were a number of students out of their classrooms at the time the alarm went off, and I will not be apportioning any blame until I have interviewed every one of them."

There was a moment's silence.

"You say it was Kelly Snier's locker you found my daughter beside this morning?" said Mrs Fox.

"Not just *beside*, Mrs Fox. Xanthe had her hand right in it. She has told me that she took Kelly's locker key in order to find something of hers that she believed Kelly had stolen, though she won't say what. And Kelly claims to have taken nothing, so it's all a bit of a mystery."

Mrs Fox glanced across at her daughter. "Xanthe? Would you care to enlighten us? What were you looking for in Kelly's locker?"

Xanthe said nothing. She just kept staring at the carpet. There was no way she was going to mention the locket in front of Mr Maguire.

"I'm afraid Xanthe's lack of co-operation is hardly helping matters here," said the headmaster. "She's not doing herself any favours."

Mrs Fox sighed. "Might I suggest that I speak to her in private and report back?" she said. "I'm quite sure I can get to the bottom of things."

"Of course," said Mr Maguire. "That's an excellent idea." He picked up a fountain pen from his desk and began twisting it between his fingers. "Excuse me for mentioning this, Mrs Fox – and do say if you'd prefer to talk to me in confidence – but I feel I must ask you something before you go."

"Yes?"

The pen turned faster in the headmaster's hand.

"It's just that – well, I couldn't help wondering whether things were all right at home. Whether there were any – er – *difficulties* I should know about."

"Meaning what exactly?" said Mrs Fox.

Mr Maguire stopped twisting the pen and clenched it in his fist. "I rather hoped *you* might be able to tell *me*," he said. "You see, until now, Xanthe has been a model student. She's always been a delight to teach and has never been in any serious trouble. Which leads me to believe there must be a reason for the change in her behaviour."

"I couldn't agree more," replied Mrs Fox. "But I strongly suspect the reason lies here at school rather than at home." She pursed her lips. "I can assure you there's nothing you need concern yourself with *there*."

Mr Maguire pushed back his chair. "I'm very glad to hear it," he said. "Very glad indeed." He got to his feet. "I'd like you to take Xanthe home now, please."

"Home?" echoed Mrs Fox, her eyes widening. "Mr Maguire, are you *suspending* my daughter?"

The headmaster shook his head. "No, no – at least, not at this stage. But I think it would be best all round if we followed your suggestion and allowed you to talk things over together in private." He crossed to the door. "Now, if you'll excuse me, I have other matters to attend to. Come and see me tomorrow morning at break, please, Xanthe. And let's hope by then you have a little more to say for yourself."

Xanthe followed her mother across the school car park.

If only her mother would *say* something, it

wouldn't be so bad. Just a few words to break the tension. But all she could hear was the click-clacking of her heels against the tarmac, punctuated by the occasional loud sniff.

She waited until her mother had unlocked the car, then slipped into the passenger seat beside her.

Mrs Fox rummaged in her bag for a handkerchief. "Oh, *Xanthe*!" she exclaimed. "Why didn't you *tell* me what was going on? Why didn't you talk to Dad and me?"

"I-I didn't want to worry you. I thought it would all blow over."

"I *knew* there was something up," went on Mrs Fox. "You were so quiet the evening of your birthday. And you weren't yourself the day before, either." She blew her nose. "So, come on. Tell me all about it. I'd like some answers, please. For a start you can tell me what you were looking for in Kelly's locker."

Xanthe flushed. "My locket."

"Your *locket*?"

"The one Grandma Alice gave me. I wore it to school yesterday, but I forgot we had hockey trials in the afternoon. I left it in my locker overnight, but when I went to get it this morning, it wasn't there."

"And you think Kelly took it?"

Xanthe nodded. "I told Grace where I was going

to put it and I think she overheard me. She must've nicked my key from my blazer while I was playing hockey and taken it then."

"And you decided to take matters into your own hands and try to get it back, did you?" asked her mother. "A pretty silly thing to do, I'd say. Getting caught with your hand in Kelly's locker when it seems you were in so much trouble already was hardly going to do you much good, was it?" She put her handkerchief back in her bag. "What about the fire alarm? I take it that *wasn't* you?"

Xanthe shook her head. "Of course it wasn't." Her eyes narrowed. "It was Kelly again, I'm sure of it. She set me up."

"And the other incidents? The things that happened in maths and science? Were they all Kelly's doing, too?"

Xanthe slumped down in her seat.

"I think so," she said. "But I can't prove any of it. Every time something goes wrong she manages to make it look like it's my fault. She's really got it in for me this term, Mum. I didn't tell you, but Saul dragged up Prize Night in front of everyone in form time on Monday, and since then it's just been one thing after another. And before you ask, I did· *try* telling Mr Maguire my side of the story on Tuesday – I told him how I reckoned it was Kelly who'd messed up my maths paper – but he said he didn't want to hear any tales. And I can't keep blaming her if I haven't got any proof, can I?"

Mrs Fox sighed. "I've got to get back to the office," she said, glancing at her watch. "I'll drop you home and we can talk more later on, OK?"

Xanthe nodded, blinking back tears. "OK. Yes, please."

Her mother's expression softened. She leaned across and gave Xanthe a hug. "Try not to worry too much, sweetheart – we'll sort things out somehow. Kelly Snier won't get away with this, I promise."

Xanthe stared miserably out of her bedroom window.

From up here she could just make out the boating lake at the far end of the park – and in front of it the boathouse itself, nestled amongst a thicket of trees. It was one of her favourite places to hang out with Grace after school, especially since bumping into Saul there last summer: they'd buy drinks at the little café near the swings and then walk round the lake, chatting and laughing. Not that they'd been there this term yet. When Grace had suggested it after art on Monday, she simply hadn't felt like it.

She lay down on her bed and closed her eyes. How was it possible for things to go so wrong in such a short space of time? What had she been thinking, snooping inside Kelly's locker like that? And why hadn't she had the sense to confide in her parents? If she'd told them everything was getting out of hand a couple of days ago, then maybe they could have helped. Maybe she wouldn't be lying here now, feeling so utterly desperate.

She rolled on to her stomach and pressed her forehead into the pillow, trying to squeeze away what felt like the stirrings of yet another headache. She hadn't mentioned those to her mother. And she hadn't mentioned the weird glowing shapes, either. She hadn't wanted to make the situation even worse.

She thought of the diary her parents had given her. Maybe Mum was right and she'd feel better if she wrote things down. Perhaps it might help her get her head straight.

Then again, it seemed a pity to spoil those lovely creamy pages with all the horrible mixed-up thoughts that were teeming through her brain. Better to wait till life improved and begin the diary on a positive note.

A loud mewing sound started up beneath her bedroom window and she got off the bed to peer outside. Her great-grandmother's cat was rubbing its sleek white body against the front door.

Xanthe trudged downstairs and opened the door a crack.

"Hello, Blanche," she murmured, looking down at the little cat. "How did you know I'd be at home? You can't come in, you know that. You'll leave your hairs all over the place and set off Dad's allergies."

The cat stared up at her with huge sapphire eyes.

Xanthe sighed. "Oh, all right, then." She opened the door a bit wider. "I suppose a very quick cuddle won't hurt. But then you'll have to go straight back to Grandma's."

She sat down on the bottom stair and settled the cat on her lap.

"I'm glad you've come, really," she murmured. "It's nice to have the company." She buried her face in the animal's soft fur, no longer able to stop the tears from running down her cheeks. "What's happening, hey? Why is everything going so wrong?"

She wiped her eyes and glanced at her watch. One forty-five. Time for afternoon lessons. At least it wouldn't be long before she'd be able to have a proper chat with Grace. So far all they'd managed was a very quick phone call and a few texts.

She pulled herself to her feet and set the cat back down on the doorstep.

"That's your lot, Blanche. Back home with you. Send my love to Grandma Alice. I'll be round to see her later."

Blanche didn't move. She just stood there on the

threshold, her tail held high. Then she began to mew again, louder this time, and more insistent.

"I said go *on*!" Xanthe bent down and gave the animal a gentle nudge, but still Blanche stayed put. "Honestly! You're not usually like this. What's got into you?"

It was then that the thought struck her.

What if this wasn't just another of Blanche's little visits? What if she had come round for a reason and was trying to tell her something?

Xanthe grabbed her keys from the table in the hallway and scooped the cat into her arms.

She shut the door behind her and hurried down the path towards the front gate.

Maybe Grandma Alice needed her.

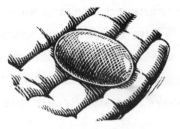

10.
The Legend of
Hildegard and Ethelfreda

Xanthe rang the doorbell, Blanche still clutched to her chest.

Perhaps Grandma Alice was ill. Or maybe she'd had a fall. A hundred terrible possibilities ran through her head as she waited on the doorstep.

"Grandma!" she exclaimed as the door opened. "Thank goodness for that! I was beginning to think…"

Blanche leaped to the ground and Xanthe hugged her great-grandmother, breathing in the familiar scent of roses on her skin.

"You were beginning to think what?" asked Grandma Alice. She pulled away and clasped Xanthe by the shoulders. "You've been crying, sweetheart. Whatever's happened?"

"Nothing," muttered Xanthe. "I just…"

"Xanthe? What's up? Why are you home at this time? And where did you find Blanche?"

Xanthe glanced down at the little cat. "She was mewing on our doorstep. I tried to get her to go home, but she wouldn't budge. She just kept on mewing, and in the end I got worried and decided to bring her back. I thought – well, I thought she might be trying to tell me there was something wrong."

Grandma Alice stooped to stroke Blanche's head. "There's nothing wrong," she said firmly. "Or at least, not with me there isn't." She straightened up and looked back at Xanthe. "Now, tell me, what are you doing home from school so early?"

Xanthe dropped her gaze. "Oh, no reason," she said. She made to turn away. "Actually, I'd better be going. I've got … er … homework and stuff to be getting on with."

Her great-grandmother reached out and put a hand on Xanthe's arm. "Oh no, you don't," she said. "Not until you've come inside and had a cup of tea, at least."

Xanthe hesitated.

"I won't take no for an answer," said Grandma Alice. She opened the front door wide and stood back to let Xanthe past. "You look like you could do with a bit of a heart-to-heart. And besides, you owe me a visit, remember?"

"Now then," said Grandma Alice, handing Xanthe a cup of tea and perching gingerly on the side of her armchair. "What about something to eat? Have you had any lunch?"

Xanthe shook her head. "Mum told me to make myself a sandwich, but I didn't really feel like it. I've – well, I've been sent home from school, you see. I've been in trouble and I…"

"Trouble?" echoed her great-grandmother. "What sort of trouble?"

Xanthe shrugged. "Trouble with Kelly. Trouble with Mr Maguire. I've been in trouble all week, really…"

"But you didn't say anything in your texts…"

"I-I didn't want to worry you…"

Grandma Alice snorted. "Don't worry about *me*." She ruffled Xanthe's hair. "Come on, sweetheart, whatever it is, you can't keep it to yourself. Bottling things up never did anyone any good."

Xanthe sighed. "All right, then," she said, her voice catching. "I suppose it *would* be good to tell you what's been going on." She sipped her tea and sat back in the armchair. "Remember what I told you when I came round on Monday? About Kelly making it look like it was me who'd thrown paint all over Miss Evans in art?"

Her great-grandmother nodded.

"Well, that was just the beginning. Since then she's been causing problems whenever she can. She played another trick on me on my birthday in maths, and then another in science on Wednesday morning, and both times she managed to make it look like it was my fault."

"Oh, Xanthe! You poor thing."

Xanthe smiled weakly. "That's not all. I've been getting horrible headaches, too. And seeing these weird glowing shapes. And then just after my piano lesson on Wednesday—" She broke off, frowning.

Grandma Alice had got up from the side of the armchair and was staring down at her.

"What is it?" asked Xanthe. "What's the matter?"

Her great-grandmother blinked. "Did I hear you right?" she said. "Did you just say you've been seeing *glowing shapes*?"

Xanthe reddened. "Sorry, I shouldn't have mentioned those. It's nothing, I'm sure…"

Grandma Alice clapped her hand to her mouth. "But that means," she murmured, "that means—"

"It doesn't mean anything, Grandma," interrupted Xanthe. "*Please* don't fret. Grace reckons I need my eyes testing, that's all."

Grandma Alice's hand fell limply to her side. "Oh, Xanthe! If only it were that simple."

"What are you talking about? I've told you, it's nothing to get stressed over. I'm sure there's a perfectly simple explanation."

Grandma Alice sank down into the armchair opposite. "What an incredibly clever cat I've got," she said, looking at Blanche. "She must have sensed we needed to talk."

Xanthe eyed her great-grandmother, but said nothing. Blanche was a pretty special cat, it was true – but she wasn't *that* clever…

"I'm going to tell you a story," said Grandma Alice. "A true story about a pair of twin sisters who lived over a thousand years ago. And I want you to listen very carefully."

"This isn't the time for stories, Grandma! Everything's going wrong in real life! And anyway, I was in the middle of telling you something."

"The twin sisters," went on Grandma Alice, ignoring her completely, "were called Hildegard and Ethelfreda, and they were as different from one another as you can possibly imagine. Ethelfreda was a sunny-tempered girl, kind and loving and everybody's favourite. Hildegard, on the other hand, was a jealous child, envious of her sister's happy-go-lucky nature and forever causing trouble. Over the years her jealousy grew, until one day she could stand Ethelfreda no longer."

She grimaced.

"The next part's a bit gruesome, I'm afraid. I think it's only best to warn you. On Midsummer's Eve, which happened to be the occasion of the twins' thirteenth birthday, Hildegard persuaded her sister to go into a nearby forest and strangled her with her own mane of chestnut hair."

Xanthe pulled a face to show she was still listening. As stories went this wasn't such a bad one, but she'd much rather have carried on talking about her terrible week at school. It would have been such a relief to get it out in the open.

Grandma Alice was leaning forwards in her armchair, her eyes bright.

"As Hildegard strangled her sister, a tremendous storm broke, unlike any that has raged before or since – and a bolt of lightning flashed in the sky above the forest, casting the shape of an X through the trees."

Xanthe put down her teacup and stared at her great-grandmother.

"The storm cleared and Hildegard fled the scene of the crime, believing herself to be rid of her sister forever. Ethelfreda's body lay undiscovered in the forest, bathed in the light of the Midsummer moon."

A smile flickered on Grandma Alice's lips. "The next day Ethelfreda rose from the forest floor, fully recovered. As she made her way home, she sensed a prickling at the back of her neck, and on later examination discovered a tiny white mark branded into her skin, just below her hairline. It was in the shape of a perfect X."

Xanthe's hand moved up towards her birthmark, her fingers shaking slightly. "Like – like me, then."

Her great-grandmother nodded.

"Exactly like you, sweetheart. And exactly like me, too."

She twisted round and lifted up her hair. Emblazoned on her skin, in precisely the same place as Xanthe's own birthmark, was a tiny white X.

Xanthe's jaw dropped.

"You, too?" she exclaimed. "But you never said. You never…" She frowned. "But I don't understand. Who *was* this Ethelfreda? And what's she got to do with you and me?"

"Oh, pretty much everything," replied Grandma Alice airily. "But I was just coming to that."

She settled back in her chair.

"By now Hildegard had discovered she had a strange new power. By focusing on a particular object, she found she could cause whatever trouble she wished. She might perhaps decide to transform the object into something different, or make it move or break. Though she did not yet know it, she had just become a Hexing Witch."

Xanthe's eyes bulged. This story was getting weirder by the minute. "A *what*?" she murmured.

"A Hexing Witch. Nasty pieces of work, Hexing Witches. No physical mark to single them out, but plenty of hidden powers nonetheless."

"Oh," said Xanthe faintly. "And – and Ethelfreda? What about her?"

"Ah, that's the good news. Ethelfreda had become a *True* Witch. A different kind of witch altogether. Someone with the power to reverse the evil deeds of Hexing Witches."

For a few seconds Xanthe sat very still, her eyes fixed on her great-grandmother. Then she threw back her head and laughed.

"Oh, Grandma!" she said. "You had me for a moment then, you really did! You got me thinking I was like this Ethelfreda character. That I was some kind of modern-day witch! You and your stories! But at least it's taken my mind off things!"

Grandma Alice looked back at her, unsmiling. "This isn't one of my 'stories', Xanthe," she said softly. "I'm sorry. It's a lot to take in, I know. I was planning to tell you everything at teatime yesterday, all nice and relaxed, but now it's come out in a bit of a rush."

A shiver snaked down Xanthe's spine.

"Have you ever wondered why you've always been so scared of fire?" her great-grandmother asked.

"Well, of course I've *wondered*…"

Grandma Alice's lips tightened. "Since ancient times, women suspected of being witches were burned at the stake," she said. "It's in our nature to fear fire. It's in our genes."

There was a very long silence.

"So I *am* like this girl in the story?" whispered Xanthe at last, her hand moving to her birthmark once more. "I'm a *witch*? We're *both* witches? We can do *magic* and stuff?"

Grandma Alice snorted.

"Magic?" she echoed. She hauled herself to her feet and motioned to Xanthe to follow her into the kitchen. "Take a look around you. Can you see any signs of magic? A bubbling cauldron on the stove, perhaps? A broomstick propped up in the corner? A spell book? A jar of pickled frogs?"

Xanthe glanced around her great-grandmother's spotless kitchen. It looked as it had always done: exceptionally neat and tidy. There was a row of terracotta pots containing coffee and teabags and sugar; a little table covered in a red-and-white checked cloth; a wooden dresser displaying an array of china. The only thing she could see that was remotely witch-like was Blanche, who had trotted after them into the kitchen and was now curled up inside her basket in the corner. But even she didn't really fit the part. Who had ever heard of a witch's cat with snow-white fur and blue eyes?

"See?" exclaimed Grandma Alice. "No evidence of magic whatsoever." She led Xanthe back into the sitting room and sat down again. "Our breed of witch doesn't do magic, Xanthe. Or at least, not the kind of magic you're thinking of."

Xanthe sank gratefully into her armchair. Her legs seemed to have turned to jelly and a thousand questions were flying round her head.

"So what *do* we do?" she asked.

"I've told you. We deal in hexes. You're a True Witch, which means you're able to reverse the hexes of Hexing Witches. That's your job. You've got the Hex Factor."

"The *Hex* Factor?"

"That's right. And very proud of it you should be, too. You come from a long and distinguished line of True Witches, Xanthe. You're one in a million. One in a *billion*, more like. Of course, there are other witches of our kind out there, both Hexing and True, created around the same time and under similar conditions – and all, of course, on their thirteenth birthdays – but the storm that broke that Midsummer's

Eve spawned only our particular line."

Xanthe gulped. "But – but how come I've never noticed anything before? How come I've always felt like an ordinary girl?"

"For the simple reason that you don't have any powers until you reach the age of thirteen," replied her great-grandmother. "It's the same with Hexing Witches. Your abilities lie silently within you. Untapped, one might say." She raised her eyebrows. "And can you honestly say you've been feeling like an ordinary girl over the past few days? What with all the trouble you've had at school and those strange glowing shapes you mentioned?"

Xanthe gripped the side of her armchair. "You mean they were to do with me being a witch?"

Grandma Alice nodded. "They're nature's way of alerting you to danger. Of telling you there's a hex about to be performed." She sighed. "Except a True Witch doesn't *usually* start seeing them until at least a month after she's turned thirteen, as she gradually acquires the powers to pick up on them from a distance. The only explanation for you seeing them so soon is that there's a Hexing Witch nearby. Though I can hardly believe it myself, there must be one at Milchester High."

Xanthe froze.

"Kelly?" she whispered.

Her great-grandmother's face grew solemn. "I don't want to jump to conclusions, and I do need to ask you a few questions about what's been going on – but yes, given her jealous nature and what you've told me so far about this week, I'm pretty sure it must be her."

"B-but that means she might be *related* to me," stammered Xanthe. "She might have inherited her powers from Ethelfreda's sister – from Hildegard."

"I suppose it's possible," replied Grandma Alice. "Though it's much more likely she's descended from a different line." She reached forward and patted Xanthe's knee. "I wouldn't get too hung up on that one if I were you. Even if she *is* from our line, you'd only be very *distantly* related."

Xanthe's heart began to pound. All those occasions over the last few days when she hadn't been able to explain things properly. All those times when things hadn't quite added up. Could it really be that Kelly was one of these Hexing Witches? And that she was using her powers to land her in trouble?

"But why haven't I been able to do anything to stop her?" she asked suddenly. "If I'm thirteen and I've come into my own powers, why haven't I been able to reverse Kelly's hexes?"

"Well, you didn't know what you were, for a start," replied her great-grandmother. "But mainly it's because you didn't have the tools. Of course, it's rather more complicated than that: there are still things I need to tell you, and so much I need to *help* you with – we need to sharpen up your powers of concentration, for example. But essentially you haven't had the wherewithal to defend yourself."

Reaching behind her, she took something from the top drawer of the bureau and held it out to Xanthe. "Here," she said. "The second part of your birthday present."

Xanthe leaned forwards. In her great-grandmother's hand lay a small flat oval of opaque crystal.

"What is it?" she asked, taking it.

"It's a piece of real moonstone," said Grandma Alice. "When Ethelfreda went into the forest that evening, she was wearing the locket she'd been given that morning for her birthday. And yes, before you ask, it's the same locket I gave to you and it's her initial engraved into the casing. Hildegard had been given one, too, but she had left hers at home, scorning the delicate piece of jewellery."

Xanthe bit her lip. Whatever else she did, she'd have to keep the bad news about the locket from her great-grandmother.

"When Ethelfreda returned home the following day," continued Grandma Alice, "her locket was no longer empty. It now contained an oval of moonstone, formed from the rays of the moon that had seeped inside the locket as she lay there on the forest floor. The rays had solidified in its base and revived her with their healing powers. Ethelfreda discovered that if she kept it close by at all times, and concentrated her energies on the glowing Xs that appeared on the objects Hildegard was hexing, she was able to reverse her sister's mischief."

Xanthe ran her finger over the milky-white oval of moonstone.

"For a while," said her great-grandmother, "the two girls remained under the same roof, Hildegard sparking hexes and Ethelfreda doing her best to reverse them. Hildegard's powers grew and grew, until one day she decided to hex her own sister. Goodness knows what would have happened if she'd succeeded, but Ethelfreda managed to summon in her defence the one and only thing she knew would terrify any witch."

"You – you're not telling me she summoned *fire*?"

Grandma Alice nodded. "It was extraordinarily brave of her. Unthinkable, really. But deep down she must have sensed it was her only weapon against her sister. It was the same with the other lines of True and Hexing Witches: soon after a pair of witches came into being, the Hexing Witch appears to have tried hexing her twin sister, and the True Witch always reacted by summoning fire."

"And what happened?" asked Xanthe.

"The Hexing Witches fled. Every one of them."

"Including Hildegard?"

"Including Hildegard. She and Ethelfreda never set eyes on one another again, though Hildegard continued to spark hexes wherever she went, and Ethelfreda found herself able to reverse them from afar, always on the alert for the telltale glowing Xs that signalled she was needed. Before long she was reversing hexes sparked by a multitude of other Hexing Witches as well."

Grandma Alice smiled to herself before going on.

"For many years Ethelfreda believed her powers would die out with her, but when her great-granddaughter was born with the same white mark on the back of her neck, she vowed to stay close to the child, sensing that one day the legacy might be passed on. Sure enough, on the occasion of the girl's thirteenth birthday, Ethelfreda's own powers vanished – and not long after that her great-granddaughter confided in her that she had seen something strange in the form of a glowing X. Ethelfreda handed over the moonstone and the locket, and told her descendant all she needed to know – and that's how it has worked ever since. The legacy skips either one or two generations, and so far it has been passed down to a girl-child in the family for nearly eleven hundred years."

Xanthe frowned. "Hang on a minute. Did you say Ethelfreda handed over the locket as well as the moonstone? Are you telling me I need that to reverse Kelly's hexes, too?"

"Oh yes. You need them both – they work together. But you've got the locket already."

The colour drained from Xanthe's face.

"Xanthe? Whatever's the matter?"

Xanthe glanced away, the back of her throat dry. "It's – it's the locket," she murmured. "I don't have it any more. Kelly stole it."

11.
The Hex Factor

"Stole it?" echoed Grandma Alice. She gaped at Xanthe. "What do you mean, *stole* it?"

Xanthe swallowed. "She – she took it yesterday afternoon. At least, I think it was her. She overheard me telling Grace I was going to leave it in my locker while I was doing the hockey trials, and I reckon she must have nicked my key from my blazer pocket and taken it then."

"She wouldn't have needed a *key* to get into your locker!" exclaimed her great-grandmother. "She would have just hexed it open. But what was the locket doing at school in the first place? I thought it was against the rules to wear jewellery."

"It is. But I reckoned if I hid it under my shirt no one would see it. I thought it might bring me luck."

117

"Luck!" cried Grandma Alice. She clasped her head in her hands. "I take it you've looked for it? In case Kelly's hidden it somewhere at school, I mean?"

"Of course I've looked for it," replied Xanthe. "That's why I've been sent home. Mr Maguire caught me poking about in Kelly's locker, and after everything else that's happened this week…"

She broke off, tears welling in her eyes.

"I'm sorry, sweetheart," said her great-grandmother. "I didn't mean to upset you. Heaven knows you've got enough to cope with right now." She patted Xanthe's arm. "Listen, why don't you begin at the beginning. Tell me when things started to go wrong."

"I've told you already. It was in art on Monday, when Kelly made me spill paint over Miss Evans. But that wasn't a hex, Grandma. It can't have been. I didn't see a glowing X."

"Ah, but you weren't thirteen on Monday, were you?"

"You mean…"

"I mean you wouldn't have seen anything if it *had* been a hex," said Grandma Alice. "Which I bet it was. Your birthday wasn't until the following day." She tapped her fingers on the side of the armchair. "Talking of birthdays, Kelly *is* thirteen, isn't she?"

"I-I think so. In fact, I'm sure of it. It was her

118

birthday over the Christmas holidays. I remember her bragging about getting to be a teenager before I did."

"Well, that makes sense," said Grandma Alice. "I expect she was just itching to get going on you the moment the new term began."

"But would she have known what I was? Would she have come back to school knowing that I was a – a witch? Is that why she chose me as her target? Or was she just picking on me because she hates me so much anyway?"

"It depends on whether she knew about your birthmark. Is that likely, d'you think?"

Xanthe shook her head. "No one knows about my birthmark at school. No one except Grace."

"Then Kelly almost certainly came back after the holidays knowing nothing about you whatsoever. She would have found out about *herself*, of course. Her Hexing Witch ancestor will have passed on the glad tidings the minute she turned thirteen." Grandma Alice shuddered. "I suppose there's a very slight chance she might know what you are *now*: if she *does* come from our ancestral line, then one glance at the locket would have told her everything – it's one of our family heirlooms, after all. But as I said, the chances of you two being related are pretty remote – and in any case, it makes little difference whether Kelly knows what you are or not: she hates you anyway, so you'll be the target of her mischief for a very long time to come – and without the locket you won't be able to do a thing about it." She sighed. "Now, come on, tell me about the rest of the week. I want to get everything straight in my head. You said Kelly played another trick on you in maths?"

Xanthe nodded.

"We were doing a test on my birthday," she said. "I was struggling with this really difficult question and just before time was up the multiplication sign started to glow. Miss Pimm made us turn over our sheets, and when she handed the tests round the class to mark, Kelly ended up with mine. The next minute she was showing Miss Pimm my paper, and when I was called up to see it, there was this massive line all the way through it and the words 'Miss Pimm's maths class stinks' scrawled in my handwriting at the bottom."

Grandma Alice clicked her tongue.

"Which you quite naturally assumed Kelly had written when she'd been given your paper?"

"Yes. Though I did think it was a bit weird how quickly she'd managed to do it. And how she'd copied my handwriting so accurately. Grace thought it was strange, too, but there didn't seem to be any other explanation."

"Ah, but there was, wasn't there?" said Grandma

Alice. "Kelly had obviously hexed your paper a few seconds before the end of the test. It was just a coincidence she got it to mark. By the time it landed on her desk, the damage had already been done." She traced the pattern on the armchair with the tip of her little finger. "Tell me, did you notice Kelly looking at you at all during the lesson?"

Xanthe considered for a moment.

"Actually, yes," she said. "Now you come to mention it, I *do* remember something. Just before I saw the sign glow someone dropped a pencil case on the floor, and when I looked up to see what was going on, I caught Kelly giving me this really dirty look. Like she was trying to stare me out."

"That would have been the moment she did it," said Grandma Alice. "Concentration is the key to everything, you see – both in the hexing and in the reversing, too. What about science? What happened there?"

"Oh, that was even worse. I had to go up and get these samples of metal, and Kelly jogged my elbow and made me drop some of them. When I got back to the workbench, Saul and I started to add the samples to test tubes of acid, and just as we were putting in the third one I saw a glowing X on the surface of the metal. There was an explosion and the test tube shattered all over the floor." Xanthe winced at the memory. "I reckoned Kelly must have taken some seriously reactive metal down from the top shelf and slipped it on to my tray while I was picking up the samples – but I guess she wouldn't have had to, would she?"

Grandma Alice shook her head.

"She'd have just hexed the metal as you were dropping it into the test tube. She could have done it from the other side of the room if she'd wanted to." She frowned. "I don't like the sound of this. Kelly's hexes are already quite sophisticated – and dangerous, too. It's one thing to make a paint pot fly up into the air – quite another to mess around with chemicals. It won't be long before she's hexing everything in sight. Including, I'm afraid, you."

"*Me?* But what do you mean?"

Grandma Alice pursed her lips.

"I mean," she said, "that with the exception of the locket and the moonstone, which a Hexing Witch can acquire only by ordinary means, nothing is beyond Kelly's reach. If she can see it, she can hex it. And with all the practice she's getting, she'll soon be strong enough to hex her ultimate prize – you."

Xanthe's eyes widened. "But Grandma! What am I going to do? How am I going to manage without the locket?"

Her great-grandmother's face crumpled. "I wish I

knew. You're not *meant* to manage without it." She sighed. "Still, at least there's one thing to be grateful for. At least Kelly hasn't got the moonstone. It's never happened before, but just think what a Hexing Witch might be able to do with that *and* the locket. The combination of the family heirlooms is incredibly powerful for *us*, after all." She wrung her hands. "Oh, Xanthe! If I'd just hung on to the locket and given it to you with the moonstone today, none of this would have happened. But I wanted you to have at least part of your inheritance on your birthday, and it didn't cross my mind there might be a Hexing Witch at your school. I mean, what were the chances of *that* happening? Hexing Witches haven't been in contact with True Witches for over a thousand years. It's rare enough for us to meet our own kind, for heaven's sake."

"So you don't know the other True Witches?"

"Oh, I know a few of them by name. But I've never had the privilege of actually meeting any of them. I don't even know how many of us there are left. Rumour has it several died at the stake during the great witch-hunts of the Reformation. And of course some die before they can pass the legacy on to their descendants."

"You mean if you'd died before I reached the age of thirteen I wouldn't have become a True Witch?"

"That's right," said Grandma Alice. "You would have kept your birthmark forever, of course. But you'd never have seen a glowing X or been able to reverse a hex. The powers within you would simply have faded away." She gazed into the distance. "I'll never forget the day you were born. What with your Aunt Becky having twin boys and Aunt Jill not wanting children, I'd pretty much given up hope of the legacy ever being passed on. And then your mother told me she was expecting a little girl, and I allowed myself the tiniest glimmer of hope. When I finally got to hold you, I had a quick peek at the back of your neck and saw that my greatest wish had come true. All I had to do was keep on going for another thirteen years." She looked back at Xanthe. "Without you the legacy would have died out forever. You were – you *are* – my only hope."

"I see," murmured Xanthe. "No pressure or anything, then." She thought for a moment. "Do I actually have any *choice* about this, Grandma? Could I just decide not to be a True Witch?"

Her great-grandmother gaped at her. "Well, you certainly don't have any choice about it *now*!" she said stiffly. "Not with Kelly after you. You're going to need all the help you can get. And surely you wouldn't *want* to turn your back on your inheritance? It's not every day a thirteen-year-old girl discovers she has hidden powers. Besides, it's your duty. It's what you've been born to do."

Xanthe reddened. "Of course it is," she said. "I'm sorry. I didn't mean to upset you." She shifted in her chair. "Anyway, you've told me about True Witches. What about Hexing Witches? Do you know how many of *those* there still are?"

"I'm afraid not. Though it's my guess there are more of them than there are True Witches. Sometimes the workload's terribly heavy. Now, finish telling me about your week, will you? Did Kelly do anything else yesterday? Before she stole the locket, I mean?"

Xanthe scowled.

"Yes, she set off the fire alarm and made it look as if it was me who'd done it." She frowned. "It's weird, though. I definitely didn't see a glowing X that time."

"Then it wasn't a hex," said Grandma Alice. "I expect Kelly's using a combination of tactics. She'll be taking great pleasure in unnerving you on every level possible."

There was a moment's silence.

"Grandma?" said Xanthe. "There's something I don't understand. Why didn't *you* pick up on these hexes of Kelly's and reverse them. You're a True Witch, after all."

Her great-grandmother let out a short laugh.

"Not any more, I'm not. Not since you turned thirteen. I might still *feel* like a True Witch, but I don't have any powers. They've all been passed on to you now."

"But surely you could have reversed the hex in art? The day before my birthday?"

"No, I couldn't have. I'd already handed the locket over to your mother, remember. In any case, I'd never have picked up on a hex that insignificant, even if I *had* still had the locket. You see, we True Witches tend to home in on only the most serious problems. Goodness knows how many low-level hexes there are going on at any one time. Hundreds and hundreds, I expect. If we allowed ourselves to focus on those, we'd never have time to reverse the ones that really mattered."

"So what sort of hexes *do* True Witches reverse?" asked Xanthe. "How nasty can Hexing Witches get?"

Grandma Alice pulled a face. "Oh, pretty nasty," she said. "They're out to cause all manner of disruption and chaos. Some are merely meddlesome, but others are vicious, intent on ruining people's pleasure for the simple reason they can't bear to see them having a good time. I once had to reverse a hex that had been sparked on a train heading for the seaside: some bitter and twisted Hexing Witch thought she'd put an end to hundreds of folk's holiday plans by derailing the carriages. Still, we stop what we can. It's not an easy job, but it's a necessary one. Without us True Witches, the world would be an even more dangerous place than it already is."

Xanthe shook her head. "Honestly, Grandma! All those times I've worried about you being bored. All those occasions I've tried to get you interested in the garden or the local needlework group. And here you were all the while, *reversing hexes*." Her eyes flitted to the television in the corner of the room. "I'm surprised you found the time to watch those TV soaps and dramas of yours."

"I didn't," replied her great-grandmother. "I haven't watched a programme on the telly for donkey's years. It was all just a cover-up. I used to start work the moment I woke up and finish well after midnight. All that concentrating took it out of me, I can tell you."

Xanthe frowned. "What did you actually see when you were picking up a hex?" she asked.

"Same as you've been seeing," replied her great-grandmother. "A glowing X smack bang in the middle of my vision."

"And what about the object that was being hexed? Did you see that clearly, too?"

"I *did* see it, but it was usually very blurry. For example, when I reversed the hex on that train, I had a vague impression of the track and the train wheels and the people inside the carriages, but not much else. It was the X that was clear and strong: that's what we True Witches have to concentrate on."

Xanthe stood up and crossed to the window. "And how am *I* supposed to do all this?" she asked, staring out into the darkening January afternoon. "Assuming I get the locket back, I mean. How am I meant to deal with all these hexes when I'm at school all week?"

Grandma Alice hauled herself out of the armchair and came to stand beside her.

"We'll find a way," she said. "It won't be easy, I grant you. But if I managed it, then you can, too. To start with, you'll probably have to do most of your hex-reversing in the evenings and weekends – but once we've sharpened up your powers of concentration you'll find you'll be able to do it pretty much any time. Of course, while I'm helping you get going we'll have to think of some story to spin your mum and dad. Tell them you're doing your homework over here or something."

"So Mum and Dad don't know anything about this at all? About me being a witch, I mean?"

Grandma Alice's eyes nearly popped out of her head. "Of course they don't!" she exclaimed. "Being *any* kind of witch is a matter of the utmost secrecy,

Xanthe. Breathe a word to anyone outside of the witching world and your powers will most likely disappear forever." She put her hand to her forehead. "Goodness me, even a retiring True Witch can't speak of the legacy until her descendant reaches the age of thirteen. Don't you think I would have told you before otherwise?"

"But they know about my birthmark…"

"Yes, yes – of course they know about your birthmark. That's why they called you Xanthe. But they don't understand its *significance*."

Xanthe was silent for a moment. "I suppose this means I can't tell Grace, either," she said at last.

"I'm afraid it does," replied Grandma Alice. "You're going to have to fib and say the glowing Xs really *were* something to do with your eyesight." She sighed. "It's hard keeping something this important from the people we're closest to. It was an absolute nightmare hiding it from my family, especially when the children were small. As for my Bill, the poor love never could understand why he came back from work most nights to find little more than soup and sandwiches on the table. But he always used to say he loved me for who I was, and as far as I was concerned, that was enough."

"I don't think I know *who* I am any more," said Xanthe. "I don't think I'll ever feel normal again."

Grandma Alice snorted. "Whatever *that* means." She squeezed Xanthe's hand. "It's a lot to take in, I realize. But you've got me to confide in, remember – and you *will* get used to it, I promise. It's just a question of taking things one step at a time." Her expression darkened. "And right now there's only one thing we need to concentrate on. We've got to get that locket back."

12.
The Secret Diary

Xanthe waved her great-grandmother a final goodbye and set off home.

She checked her watch. Nearly four-thirty. She'd been with Grandma Alice not quite three hours, yet in that time everything had changed.

In her clenched hand lay the moonstone, its smooth hardness a comfort against her flesh. *Look after it, whatever you do,* her great-grandmother had warned her before she'd left just now – and Xanthe had seen the panic in her eyes as she'd said it. *Of course, I never expected you'd need to take it into school – but you'll have to now. Keep it close by at all times, but make sure it's out of sight. The last thing we want is for Kelly to get hold of that as well.*

Grandma Alice had given her a photo, too – taken

of the two of them last summer. *For public show,* she had explained. *People expect there to be something inside a locket, so if you do manage to get it back, this is to go over the moonstone.*

Xanthe rounded the corner and glanced up the road. It looked like Mum was home from work already. Her car was parked outside the house, and though it wasn't quite dark yet, one or two lights had been switched on downstairs.

Usually she loved it when Mum got back early. She'd break off from her homework and they'd sit together in the kitchen, chatting over mugs of tea. Today, though, she'd have given anything to have returned to an empty house. She needed time to herself, just to sit and think.

She slid her key into the lock and pushed open the front door. From the kitchen she could hear her mother talking on the phone. She could buy herself a few minutes' peace and quiet, at least.

Xanthe crept up the stairs and tiptoed into her room. She shut the moonstone inside her desk, then sat down on the bed and reached for her mobile.

Her spirits rose. She had ten messages – and the first was from Grace. Maybe she'd found the locket...

But she was only sending her love and promising to ring later when she was back from her dance class. All the other messages were from people pulling out of her party. Tilly Wilson had obviously started a trend: it definitely wasn't cool to mix with a troublemaker.

Xanthe put down her mobile and sighed. Soon it wouldn't be worth *having* a party.

There was a knock at the bedroom door and her mother came in. "Hi," she said. "I managed to get away early. I thought you might be in need of that chat." She gave Xanthe a hug. "Been round at Grandma Alice's, have you?"

Xanthe nodded.

"I thought as much. She can always be counted on to cheer you up. I bet she had a word or two to say about Kelly Snier!"

You could say that, thought Xanthe to herself.

Her mother sat down next to her. "I've been thinking, sweetheart, and I reckon I've come up with a bit of a plan."

Xanthe eyed her mother. "What kind of a plan?"

"Well, I wondered what you thought about me taking the morning off work tomorrow and us going to see Mr Maguire together. From what you've said, you've been so worried about him calling you a tell-tale, you haven't really given your side of the story at all. With me beside you, you might find it easier to explain how Kelly's had a problem with you ever since Prize Night – and how things have escalated this term—"

"*No way!*" interrupted Xanthe, rising to her feet.

Her mother stared at her. "What d'you mean, *no way?*"

Xanthe opened her mouth to speak, then shut it again. She sank back down on to the bed.

How was she supposed to explain that this was the *last* thing they should do? Mr Maguire would almost certainly call Kelly into the office and try to thrash things out between them: and *then* what would happen? Kelly would redouble her efforts to make life difficult, that's what. She'd probably start sparking hexes in every lesson. It didn't bear thinking about.

"You seemed glad of the support earlier on," remarked her mother, a little huffily.

"I *am* glad of the support. Of course I am. But I've had a chance to think things through, too – and I reckon I'd prefer to fight my own battles, if that's OK with you."

Her mother raised her eyebrows. "You don't seem to be fighting this one very well."

There was a short silence.

"*Please* leave things to me, Mum," said Xanthe. "I've got to go and see Mr Maguire at break tomorrow anyway, haven't I? Maybe I'll try explaining things to him then. But let me do this by myself. Give me till the end of tomorrow, at least. We can discuss it again over the weekend." She glanced away before going on. "Talking of the weekend, there's something I need to tell you."

"Yes?"

"I've had a load of messages from people cancelling on me this Saturday."

"*Cancelling* on you?"

"Tilly Wilson started it all off," explained Xanthe. "She's a bit of a goody-goody, and it looks like she's managed to persuade quite a few of the girls in my class that it's not cool to hang out with someone who's spent the best part of the week in the headmaster's office."

Her mother gaped at her.

"Anyway," went on Xanthe, "Anna's pulled out now, and so have Pippa and Gabby. And five or six others. Most of the boys are still planning on coming, I guess. Though I'm pretty sure Saul won't be…"

"Why not?"

Xanthe swallowed. "Because of what happened in science. I don't think he wants anything more to do with me."

"So much for friendship," muttered Mrs Fox. She thought for a moment. "So who's left, then? Who *is* coming to this party?"

Xanthe shrugged. "Like I said, most of the boys. And three girls, if you count Grace. Oh, and possibly Donna."

"Donna?"

"She's new. I thought it'd be nice to include her, though when I mentioned it, she didn't seem too keen. Still, who can blame her? She's hardly going to want to get mixed up with the class troublemaker, is she?"

"But you're *not* the class troublemaker! Nothing could be further from the truth. Up till now, no one's ever had a bad word to say about you." Mrs Fox pursed her lips. "Tell you what, why don't I ring round some of the parents and try to set the record straight? The ones I know, at least. I'm sure they'll understand if I explain…"

"Mum!" exclaimed Xanthe. "Don't even think about it! I'm not a little kid any more! Just leave things alone, will you? If anyone else cancels we might have to call the whole thing off, but let's wait and see, OK?"

Her mother frowned. "You do seem to be taking this very well," she said, getting to her feet. "Almost *too* well. Though I suppose all this business at school won't exactly be putting you in a party mood."

"Something like that," said Xanthe.

Mum was right. She wasn't in a party mood. Quite honestly, she couldn't care less if Saturday night was cancelled or not.

She had rather more important things to worry about.

Xanthe sat up in bed and gazed into the darkness.

It was no use. She might as well give up on getting any sleep tonight. There was too much stuff teeming round her brain.

It was difficult to know which was worse: being alone like this with nothing but a jumble of confused thoughts for company, or downstairs with her parents, locked into some impossible conversation where one side simply didn't know all the facts.

Tomorrow was going to be even harder. For the first time ever she wouldn't be able to confide in her best friend. It had been bad enough earlier on when Grace had rung up to talk about what had happened at school. The one thing she ached to tell her, she couldn't. And that made her feel like just about the loneliest person in the world.

Xanthe hugged her knees to her chest.

At least she'd persuaded her parents to keep out of things for now. When her father had got home from work that evening, he'd been all for going along with Mum's plan to see Mr Maguire together in the morning. He'd even offered to come with them.

She could picture the scene: she and Mum and Dad sitting one side of Mr Maguire's desk, raking over all the occasions Kelly had been unpleasant to her.

She would sit there cringing while her parents tried to argue her case, and then Kelly would be called into the office and asked for her side of the story. By first lesson she'd have hexes flying at her from every direction. By break she'd be dead meat.

Xanthe pulled the duvet round her. Somehow she'd managed to talk them out of it. She'd spun them some line about being a teenager now and having to stand on her own two feet, and they'd seemed to buy it. They'd even looked quite proud. Not that it counted for anything. She wasn't feeling in the least bit brave at the moment, and if someone had come along offering the right kind of help, she would have grabbed it with both hands. It was just that Mum and Dad were offering about the worst kind of help possible.

What she would have given to go back to being the girl she'd been a week ago. Or *thought* she'd been. Right now she didn't care if she didn't shine at anything much at school, that she was hopeless at things like maths and science. All she wanted was to be a normal teenager.

She cast her mind back to the speech she'd made in class at the beginning of the week. What was it Mr Wood had said to her afterwards? Something about art, wasn't it? Yes, that was it. *It sounds like art is what you've been born to do.*

A wave of nausea swept through her. How would she find time to devote herself to art now? According to Grandma Alice, she'd been born to save the world from the wicked deeds of Hexing Witches, not while away the hours with a sketch pad and a box of watercolours. And that was the very *best* she could hope for – that was assuming she got the locket back.

Xanthe turned on the bedside lamp, tears streaking her face. As she reached for a tissue, her fingers brushed against the diary she had been given on her birthday.

Picking it up, she unlocked the tiny gold padlock.

Would it be against the rules to confide in the diary? Surely not. Grandma had said she mustn't *speak* to anyone about the legacy, hadn't she? She hadn't said anything about writing things down.

Xanthe pushed back the duvet and got out of bed. She crossed over to her desk and rummaged around in the drawer for something to write with. A pencil would be best – less definite than pen, somehow. She wasn't ready to set all this out in ink just yet.

She chose the softest pencil she could find and padded back to bed.

How should she begin? There was so much to get out of her head and on to the page: the legend of Hildegard and Ethelfreda; the glowing Xs; the moonstone; the locket… At this rate she'd be writing all night long.

She positioned the pencil over the top of the page.

When it came down to it, only one thing really mattered, didn't it?

Friday, 10th January, she wrote. *Today I found out that I am a witch.*

13.
Outcast

A hush descended over the playground as Xanthe walked through the school gates. Everyone stopped what they were doing and stared at her. A group of Year Nines started whispering amongst themselves, and some Year Seven girls standing near the main entrance nudged each other and giggled nervously.

It was even worse with the Year Eights. Grace wasn't in yet and neither, thank goodness, was Kelly. But when she tried to catch Saul's eye, he simply turned his back on her, and several members of her class went past without saying a word. True, some of them shot her sympathetic looks, but they didn't come over and say anything. There was no doubt about it: overnight she'd become a social outcast.

Xanthe traced her finger over the outline of the

moonstone, which she'd zipped inside her skirt pocket. She would have preferred to have left it behind at home, but Grandma Alice had insisted she keep it with her at all times.

She felt a surge of relief as she saw Grace hurry in through the gates.

"Xanthe!" exclaimed Grace as she approached. "It's brilliant to have you back!" She put down her bag and gave her friend a hug. "Is there any more news on the party?"

"It's off," said Xanthe. "Three of the boys left messages cancelling last night. Even Mum couldn't see the point in trying to rescue things after that."

Grace's eyes widened. "That's awful! You must be gutted."

"I'll get over it. It's not exactly the most important thing in the world, is it?"

"Yeah, but you were looking forward to it so much…"

"I can't have a party when no one wants to come near me, can I?" reasoned Xanthe. She gestured around the playground. "Look at them all, Grace. Anyone'd think I had the plague."

Grace followed her gaze.

"So, what are we going to do about tomorrow, then?" she said at last. "We can still celebrate, surely? Hayley hasn't cancelled, has she? Or Emma?

We could come round to your place. Order in some pizza and watch a film, maybe?"

Xanthe shrugged.

"If you want," she said.

Grace frowned. "This isn't about what *I* want," she said. "It's about what *you* want. I'm trying to think of ways to make things better for you."

"Then help me find my locket. That's the only thing I'm bothered about right now."

Grace's face fell. "Oh, Xanthe. I thought after what happened yesterday you'd have given up on that for now."

"*Given up on it?* You must be joking! I've absolutely got to find it. I've got to find it *today*."

Grace put a hand on her friend's arm. "OK … OK… Calm down. I only meant you don't want to be getting yourself into even worse trouble than you're in already."

"I couldn't be in any worse trouble if I tried…"

"Oh, but you could!" exclaimed Grace. "Of course you could! They could expel you, for a start." The bell rang and she picked up her bag. "I know you must be worried about what your great-grandma will say if you have to tell her you've lost it, but if she knew the trouble you were getting yourself into trying to get it back, I bet you anything she'd tell you to forget all about it."

Xanthe raised her eyebrows. She hitched her bag on to her shoulder and followed Grace towards the main entrance.

"And *I* bet you anything she wouldn't."

Xanthe sat down and waited for Grace to come back from the cloakroom. History would start in a few minutes and she was saving her friend the seat next to her. Not that it looked like anyone else was in much of a hurry to keep her company.

She allowed herself a small sigh of relief. She'd managed to get through the whole of English without anything bad happening. Still, that was only because Kelly hadn't put in an appearance yet. According to Mr Wood, she was at the dentist's and wouldn't be in till just before break.

She looked up to find Donna standing beside her.

"Oh, hi," she said, smiling. "How are you?"

Donna blushed. "I'm OK," she murmured, fiddling with her long brown hair. "Er – about your party – I'd like to come, if that's still all right with you."

Xanthe's face fell. "Oh, Donna!" she exclaimed. "I'm afraid it's been called off. Loads of people have cancelled on me – because of all the trouble I've been in this week. I thought you might have heard."

Donna shook her head.

"But why don't you come round anyway?" rushed on Xanthe. "Grace thought we could order in a pizza and watch a film. You'd be more than welcome to join us. There'll probably be a couple of others there, too." She scribbled something on a scrap of paper and handed it to Donna. "Here's my number. Ring me if you feel like coming and I'll give you directions."

Donna stared down at the piece of paper. "Thanks," she said. "I might just do that." She turned to go back to her seat.

"It'd be great if you could," called Xanthe after her.

Donna glanced round at her and nodded. "Like I said, thanks for the invitation."

"It's a pleasure," replied Xanthe.

And she meant it, too. It was nice to do something right for a change.

Just before break the door opened and Kelly walked into the classroom.

Every muscle in Xanthe's body stiffened.

"Sorry, Mr Shorthouse," said Kelly, beaming at the history teacher. "I've been at the dentist's."

Mr Shorthouse looked up from the whiteboard.

"Yes, OK – come and sit down, Kelly. You'll have to borrow someone else's work and copy up later on."

Xanthe watched as Kelly made her way to one of the spare seats and began rummaging around inside her bag.

She'd expected her to look different today, somehow. Now that she knew what Kelly actually was, she'd thought there would be something distinctive about her, something *other*. But she looked just as she'd always done: the same long blonde hair, the same icy blue eyes, the same arrogant expression.

She sighed. Another couple of minutes and Mr Maguire would be expecting her in his office for their breaktime chat. She wasn't exactly looking forward to it, but at least it would keep her away from Kelly for a bit longer, and at least on the way she'd get the chance to think about how she might get her locket back.

"Xanthe! Will you please look at the board and concentrate!" Mr Shorthouse had twisted round from the whiteboard and was glaring at her, his thick black eyebrows drawn together. "And Kelly, too! Stop fiddling with your bag and listen. There's no point getting your books out now. Like I said, you can copy up after the lesson."

He returned his attention to the whiteboard and started explaining the bullet points he had just written up.

Xanthe forced herself to look straight ahead …
but she couldn't focus on a word Mr Shorthouse was
saying. Inside Kelly's half-open bag she could have
sworn she'd just seen something glint. Could it have
been the locket?

The bell rang and people began scraping back
their chairs and streaming out of the classroom.

Xanthe picked up her books and turned to Grace.
"I'll see you later, then," she said, one eye on Kelly,
who was bending down beside her bag. "I'll come
and find you once I've been to see Mr Maguire."

"Don't you want me to walk with you to his
office?"

"No … no … I'm OK by myself, really."

Grace frowned. She looked around the classroom.
Apart from herself and Xanthe, only Kelly remained.
"What are you up to?" she whispered. "You're
plotting something, aren't you?"

"Of course I'm not. Please, Grace. Just get off to
break and leave me to it."

"But—"

"I'll be fine, *honestly…*"

Grace shrugged and made her way out of the
classroom, glancing over her shoulder as she went.

Xanthe swallowed. Perhaps she was mad to
confront Kelly now. Perhaps it would be better to
hold on till lunch and find a way to look inside her

bag then. But what if Kelly had sparked another hex on her by that time and she'd been sent home from school again? That wouldn't be much use, would it? No, she needed to grab the chance while she had it. Slowly she advanced towards Kelly.

"Xanthe!" Kelly looked up in surprise. Her face twisted into a snide grin. "Made it to break without getting into trouble, have you?"

Xanthe didn't reply. She waited until she was standing directly over Kelly, then swooped down and plunged her hand inside her bag.

"Hey! What d'you think you're doing?" cried Kelly, tugging it away. "Get off my bag…"

Xanthe lunged once more.

"I said get *off*!"

"Only if you give me back my locket…"

Kelly stared up at her, her eyes glinting.

Xanthe's heart missed a beat. *Kelly was about to hex her…*

She forced herself to stare back, white-hot anger coursing through her veins.

"Go on, stare away!" she cried. "I know what you're doing! I–I know what you *are*!" She caught hold of Kelly's collar and pulled her towards her. "But you don't scare me. You never have done and you never will do…"

"Girls!"

They turned as one, Xanthe's hand still grasping Kelly's collar. Standing at the open door was Mr Wood, his face aghast.

"Xanthe, what on earth do you think you're doing?" he exclaimed. "Let go of Kelly this instant!" He beckoned them both towards him. "Dust yourselves down, the pair of you! You're coming with me!"

14.
The Tryst

Xanthe stared out of the car window.

She didn't think she'd ever seen her mother so angry before in her life. Since picking her up from school ten minutes ago she hadn't uttered a single word, and it didn't take a genius to work out why. If there was one thing Mum hated it was violence. Slanging matches were just about OK, but actual fighting – even if it was only grabbing someone by the collar – was strictly off limits. That kind of behaviour was for animals, not human beings, she'd always said.

Xanthe cast her mind back over the last hour: the confrontation between her and Kelly; the long silent walk to Mr Maguire's office with Mr Wood; and then yet another interview with the head. It had all passed in a kind of haze, as if it were happening to somebody else.

Of course, she should never have lost her temper, she knew that. But back there in the classroom it had been impossible to think straight. All she'd known was that Kelly was seconds away from hexing her, and that knowledge had stirred such anger inside her that for a few terrible moments she had completely lost control.

Mr Wood had marched them both to Mr Maguire's office and left Kelly sitting outside while he'd taken Xanthe in to see the headmaster. The interview hadn't lasted long. As far as Mr Maguire was concerned Xanthe had crossed some invisible line of conduct, and was no longer welcome at Milchester High: for the time being, at least, she was suspended. Ten minutes later her mother had arrived, and soon after that she'd found herself being driven through the school gates, perhaps never to return.

Xanthe bit her lip.

One thing made her blood boil. As she'd left the headmaster's office, she had caught sight of Kelly, who was still sitting outside. She was doing a grand job of playing the wronged victim, all tear-stained face and shocked expression, but as Xanthe had passed she had glanced up at her for the briefest of seconds and winked.

She clenched her fists.

At least she'd avoided being hexed. At least she could be grateful for that. Though when she thought about it, that didn't really count for much. She was doing a good enough job of getting herself into trouble right now without Kelly's help.

So far Mum had managed to keep up the silence for over two hours. At lunchtime she'd fixed them both a sandwich and taken hers out into the garden, where she'd been working ever since they'd got home. Xanthe could see her from her bedroom window, jabbing at the frosty ground with a fork.

The last thing she'd wanted to do was upset her mother. They hardly ever fell out, and on the rare occasion they did, it was always because Xanthe had disappointed her in some way. That was the trouble with having no brothers or sisters: her parents only had her to pin their hopes and dreams on.

It would have been so much better if Mum had just dropped her at home and gone straight back to work. That way both of them would have had a bit of breathing space. And that way she wouldn't be stuck here like this, unable to do anything much except sit around answering Grace's increasingly anxious texts. Mum hadn't actually said she was grounded – she hadn't said anything at all – but it was pretty obvious she wasn't going to allow her out this afternoon.

Her mobile beeped and she checked the screen. At once her pulse quickened. It was Saul's number. She hadn't seen that for a good few days.

Kelly's confessed to setting off the fire alarm, the message read. *I owe you a BIG apology. Realize you've been telling the truth all along. And I've found your locket. No time to explain. Meet me after school at the boathouse. Saul*

Xanthe's jaw dropped. Saul had found her locket! Grace must have confided in him, and he'd actually cared enough to look for it. What was more, he wanted to hand it over to her in person – and in private, too.

She stared at his name at the end of the text and felt herself blush. Usually he just put a smiley face: this felt altogether more serious.

I'll be there, she typed back, trying to stop her hands from shaking. *I'll see you as close to 4 as I can make it. And THANK YOU!*

She pressed the send button and closed her eyes.

Already her heart felt lighter than it had done in days. In a few short minutes she'd got both Saul and her locket back.

Now all she had to deal with was Mum.

Xanthe waited until the car had disappeared in the direction of the shops, then slipped her mobile into her coat pocket and ran downstairs.

Letting herself out of the front door, she allowed herself a small grin.

Thanks to Grandma Alice, it had all gone exactly as planned. As soon as she'd replied to Saul, she'd texted her great-grandmother and filled her in on the day's events. Up till then she hadn't felt in the least like getting in touch, but Saul's message had changed everything. A few minutes later she'd heard the phone ring downstairs, and then Mum had broken her silence to come and tell her that she'd be going out later on for an hour or so. Grandma Alice urgently needed some shopping done.

Xanthe hurried down the path towards the front gate. The sky was thick with clouds and a few flakes of snow had started to fall.

She crossed the road at the top of the hill and looked down over the park towards the boathouse. It was sweet of Saul to suggest meeting there. Perhaps he remembered that day last summer, too – when he'd run into her and Grace at the edge of the lake. They'd had such a brilliant time, messing about in the sunshine and laughing their heads off at Saul almost capsizing the boat with his over-enthusiastic pedalling.

From inside her pocket her mobile beeped.

It was another message from Grace.

Ring me when you get this! Loads to tell! x

She turned her mobile on to silent and put it back inside her pocket. She'd ring Grace later. Most likely she knew about Saul finding the locket and wanted to fill her in on the details, but that conversation could wait.

Xanthe reached the bottom of the hill and passed through the front gates of the park. It was deserted, save for a group of runners and a young mother pushing a pram, a grizzling toddler at her heels.

She walked past the café and the swings and the little wooden bandstand, and headed for the boathouse, shrouded in its thicket of trees. She could see its outline now, and through the trees a flash of silver and red: the familiar colours of the Milchester High uniform.

She quickened her pace, her spirits soaring as she covered the final distance.

And then a figure stepped out from between the trees and she opened her mouth to call out Saul's name.

But it wasn't Saul.

It was Donna.

15.
The Lake

"Donna?" Xanthe skidded to a halt, her forehead creasing into a frown. "What are *you* doing here? I – I was expecting Saul."

Donna stared straight at her. Her face was as pale as ever, but it had lost its shyness and now there was a mocking look in her eyes.

"Amazing what you can do with somebody else's mobile," she said, slipping her hand into her coat pocket and pulling something out.

Xanthe blinked. She'd recognize that phone anywhere. Saul had got it for his birthday last year: it was the very latest model, and his pride and joy. "He-he lent it to you?" she stammered.

"Not exactly *lent*," replied Donna.

"You mean you *nicked* it?"

"Let's just say I borrowed it. I needed to get in touch with you rather urgently."

Xanthe gazed back at Donna through the falling snow. She felt as though a thick fog had wrapped itself around her brain. Nothing was making the slightest bit of sense.

"Oh!" she exclaimed, the fog lifting a little. "You mean you wanted to talk to me about tomorrow? About my birthday?" She glanced down at Saul's phone. "But don't you have a mobile of your own?"

"Of course I didn't want to talk to you about your *birthday!*" replied Donna. She shuddered. "Just the thought of spending the evening with you makes my skin crawl. I reckoned I was going to *have* to come in order to get what I needed, but as soon as you started rabbiting on about it to me this morning, I knew I couldn't bring myself to do it. And I knew I couldn't wait that long, either."

Xanthe's eyes widened. The fog was back: and it was even thicker than before.

"You still don't get it, do you?" went on Donna, shaking her head. "You really are as stupid as you look. *I* sent you that text, Xanthe. I sent it from Saul's mobile. I wanted you to think it was from him."

"But why would you want to pretend to be Saul? Did he tell you to come here? Have you – have you got my locket?"

Donna leaned back against the trunk of a nearby tree and folded her arms.

"Ah," she said. "The locket. We'll come to that in a minute. Seems there are a few things you need to understand first." She ran her finger over Saul's mobile. "Like why I'm here, for a start."

Something began to tug at the edges of Xanthe's mind. What was it Donna had just said about tomorrow evening? *I reckoned I was going to have to come in order to get what I needed.*

"Think about it, Xanthe. Think what I might want from you."

And now the fog was clearing and everything was slotting into place like the pieces of a jigsaw.

"*You?*" Xanthe gaped at Donna. "You're the Hexing Witch? But – but I thought it was Kelly."

Donna laughed. "That girl's been more useful than I can say. Ever since my first day when I got caught up in that pathetic argument by the lockers, I knew I was on to a good thing. Kelly was the perfect foil for what I wanted to achieve."

Xanthe's heart slammed against her chest.

"Not that I knew what you *were* back then," continued Donna. "It wasn't till Wednesday afternoon, when I heard you and your sad little sidekick talking in the changing room I realized *that*. Up till then I thought you were just an annoying goody-goody."

She curled her lip at Xanthe.

"Honestly, that speech you gave on Monday! All that nonsense about losing yourself in your painting! You had Mr Wood eating out of your hand, didn't you?" Her eyes narrowed. "You're not the only person who's good at art – I was top of my year at my old school. It's just that we don't *all* go around bragging about it."

"So you thought you'd teach me a lesson," said Xanthe quietly. "And hex the pot of paint in art."

"Got it in one. And it was so easy, too. From where I was sitting I had an uninterrupted view of you." Donna grinned. "I could see that Kelly was causing you trouble, twisting the paint pot round and round, and it seemed too good an opportunity to miss. I just needed to wait for the right moment."

Xanthe swallowed, remembering all too well the terrible image of her paint-splattered teacher.

"The look on your face when the paint landed on Miss Evans!" exclaimed Donna. "The look on *all* your faces! But then what happened? Your favourite teacher let you off with a mere telling-off. Talk about teacher's pet!" She sighed. "After that, hexing anyone else was out of the question until I'd put you in your place."

Xanthe said nothing.

"My chance came the very next day. I was sitting

only a few tables away from you in maths and my sight line was perfect. The only trouble was that Miss Pimm was watching everyone like a hawk." Donna frowned. "I'm going to have to be careful with her. She doesn't take any prisoners. Anyway, I thought if I could just create some kind of disturbance, I'd be able to distract her, so I—"

"I know what you did," interrupted Xanthe. "You dropped your pencil case."

Donna raised her eyebrows.

"Waking up a bit now, aren't you?" she said. "Perhaps you're not *quite* so stupid after all." She smirked. "That's right, I pushed my pencil case over the side of the desk, and poor old Pimmface had to grovel around picking everything up, giving me the chance to concentrate my energies on you. I timed it to perfection: just before the end of the test, I hexed your paper – a nice thick line down the middle of it and a few choice words at the bottom in your handwriting."

Xanthe dug her nails into the palms of her hands.

"When Kelly got your paper to mark I could hardly believe my luck – it was easy to see where you'd lay the blame. And to top it all, I could see that Saul was starting to lose his faith in you. I couldn't wait for another opportunity, especially now I realized how useful Kelly was turning out to be."

Donna smiled to herself.

"The next morning I saw you and Saul making up in the playground, and that made me even more determined. Why should someone as plain and boring as you get all his attention? He's way too good for you." She turned Saul's phone around in her hand, flushing slightly. "I can't wait to earn myself a few brownie points tomorrow by 'pretending' I've found this. He's been so friendly and welcoming to me." Her voice hardened. "And so *helpful*, too. It was thanks to him I discovered this place was one of your favourite after-school haunts."

Xanthe pressed her nails even harder into her flesh.

"Anyhow, I reckoned it would only take one more mess-up on your part to undo all that sickly making-up. I just needed to get you both into trouble, and make Saul think you were to blame. I was going to hang on till later in the day, but then Saul changed his mind about being my lab partner in science, and I decided I couldn't wait." Donna ran her fingers through her hair. "I don't mind admitting I was nervous. Obviously I've been practising transforming things at home, but turning a piece of zinc into a seriously reactive metal is hardly hexing for beginners. I was *so* pleased when it worked. That explosion gave me a real taste of

161

what I'll be able to do in the future." She gave an exaggerated sigh. "Of course you blamed that one on poor Kelly, too – and all because she happened to jog you when you were collecting the samples. Like I said, she really has proved to be the most brilliant foil."

Xanthe pushed her hands into her coat pockets. Around them the light was starting to fade and the snow was falling more heavily, covering the ground in white.

"What about the fire alarm?" she said. "Was that you, too?"

Donna shook her head. "Don't be stupid!" She shivered. "No – turns out it really *was* Kelly that time. She's confessed to the headmaster. She must have realized after science that you were close to landing yourself in serious trouble and decided to give you a helping hand."

"She didn't take the locket, though, did she?" said Xanthe. "It must've been something else I saw in her bag this morning. You stole it – after you heard me in the changing rooms telling Grace where I'd put it."

"That's right," said Donna. She sniggered. "When I think of all the trouble you got into for stealing Kelly's key! And all the while I'd simply hexed the locker open!"

She moved a step closer to Xanthe.

"Which brings me rather neatly to why I'm here," she said, her breath clouding on the frosty air. "You see, I think you might have something else that interests me. Something that fits inside the locket? A piece of moonstone, perhaps?"

Xanthe froze.

"Yes, I'm afraid we *are* related," went on Donna. "I'm descended from the great Hildegard, and I know all about the legend." She pulled a face. "I don't like it much, either. The thought of being related to someone as annoying as you makes me feel physically sick."

Xanthe felt her guts twist inside her.

"Imagine my surprise when I found the locket was empty. I mean, what sort of a half-witted witch would pass down only part of their descendant's inheritance?"

"Don't you dare criticize my great-grandmother!" cried Xanthe.

Donna raised her eyebrows.

"Touchy, aren't we?" she said. "Well, all I can say is that she sounds a lot less clued-up than *my* great-grandmother."

Xanthe glared back at her. A worm of anger had stirred somewhere deep inside her, and it was starting to inch its way to the surface.

"Anyway," went on Donna, "I could only assume that the reason there was no moonstone inside the locket was that she was taking her time explaining things to you. Perhaps she was worried it would all come as a bit of a shock to her poor, shy little Xanthe. But surely she's handed it over by *now*? After the week you've had, she'd have been mad not to."

Xanthe stuck out her chin. "And what if I *have* got the moonstone? What's it to you?"

Donna shrugged. "I just thought we could do a bit of a deal, that's all. If you give it to me, I promise to leave you alone. True, you'll be stripped of your powers forever, but at least you can go back to being the dull Xanthe Fox you always were – and you'll be safe in the knowledge I'll never hex you again."

Xanthe let out a short laugh. Did Donna honestly think she was going to fall for that? All she'd be doing by surrendering the moonstone would be risking handing over untold powers. In any case, who was Donna to tell her who she wanted to be? Whether she got the locket back or not, the girl she had been was gone forever – and maybe that wasn't such a bad thing after all. Standing here right now, her head clear and the blood pumping through her veins, she felt more sure of herself than she'd ever done before.

"I'm warning you," said Donna, "I'll make your

life hell if you don't give me that moonstone. And don't tell me you haven't got it, because I won't believe you."

She moved closer.

"Come on, Xanthe, this witching business isn't for you. You're not cut out for it. Think of all the things you could do instead. Think of your *art*."

Xanthe's eyes blazed. How dare Donna try to tell her what she could and couldn't do? It was *her* life. If she'd been born to be a True Witch – well, then that was what she'd be. As for her art, she'd find time for that, too. Nothing was impossible.

They were so close now she could see the specks of grey in Donna's eyes, feel her breath against her skin. And then she saw it … a flash of silver chain half hidden under the folds of Donna's scarf.

She pounced, tearing at the scarf and clawing at the chain beneath.

"Give … me … back … my … locket!"

Donna cried out, staggering backwards against the weight of Xanthe's fury. Together they stumbled through the snow-flecked thicket of trees, locked in an embrace … past the boathouse and straight out on to the little jetty jutting out over the lake.

Too late they saw where they were heading … too late the black water loomed up before them … too late they tried to jerk back from the edge…

For a split second they hung there, poised like a pair of dancers attempting some impossible move – and then they lurched sideways, fracturing the crust of ice as they fell and disappearing into the lake's murky depths.

16.
Fire

Xanthe's first thought as she plummeted through the water was how silent everything was. Her second was that the cold had completely numbed her. It had to be close to freezing down here, yet her body felt quite comfortable – warm, even. Slimy tendrils of weed brushed against her face and tangled themselves round her arms and legs, but she was no longer clinging to Donna. The fall must have knocked them apart.

A surge of panic rushed through her. *She was running out of air…*

Opening her eyes against the greyness, she thrust upwards with all four limbs. If she could just fill her lungs again, then she could get back to the edge of the lake, she was sure of it. She'd always been a strong swimmer.

Any moment now she would be bursting into the snowy half-light of the January afternoon... Any moment now she would be helping herself to mouthfuls of delicious oxygen...

But instead she bumped against something hard and unyielding. As she stretched up her hand and felt the slippery smoothness above her head, she knew in an instant what it was.

Ice! She'd forgotten all about the ice! Everything had happened so fast up there that she'd scarcely noticed the surface splinter as she and Donna had plunged into the lake.

Xanthe scrabbled around for a break in the frozen ceiling, her lungs shrivelling up inside her like deflating balloons. Surely she had to be close to the place where they had broken through...

She balled her hands up into fists and began punching at the ice, but it wasn't so easy to rupture from below, and all she could hear was an eerie creaking as it shifted and settled above her.

Darkness was starting to creep over her ... her chest was constricting ... and now something was wrapping itself round one of her legs and dragging her back down...

She kicked out with the other leg, thinking at first that she had become entangled in some giant piece of weed. But weed wouldn't tug at her like this, surely? Only a human being could pull with such determination – and the only other human being down here was Donna…

Xanthe opened her mouth to cry out – and in the same instant knew she was finished. In a few moments she would lose all sensation: her lungs would fill with water and darkness would overwhelm her completely.

Two seconds passed … three … four … yet still she could feel the tightness around her leg, still she could feel herself being dragged towards the bottom of the lake. What was more, the constriction in her chest was easing, the suffocating darkness was lifting like a veil and beneath her she could just make out the shadowy outline of Donna's figure.

And then it struck her.

She was breathing underwater… Her mouth was wide open and she was sucking in the water in great greedy gulps, pulling it down into her lungs as if it was air.

The grip round her legs loosened and Donna appeared beside her, grabbing her by the shoulders and staring into her face.

"You didn't know, did you?" she smirked, holding Xanthe down and treading water. "You didn't know you could breathe down here? Honestly! Haven't you been taught anything?"

Xanthe gaped back at her. How was this possible? Not only could she breathe, she could hear every word Donna was saying...

"Witches don't drown, stupid. That's one of the things that marks us out. Water's a natural medium for us — as natural as air. That's why you won't be feeling the cold."

Xanthe tried to calm herself. It was too much to take in. Grandma Alice had said there were things she still needed to explain, but she'd thought she'd meant all that stuff about sharpening up her powers of concentration. She'd never imagined *this*.

"Not that I would have *chosen* a place like this to finish our little conversation," went on Donna, her brown hair streaming out behind her. "It won't be much fun getting out. You'll be frozen half to death by the time you get back home." She paused for a second. "*If* you get back home."

She tightened her grasp round Xanthe's shoulders. "I'm afraid the game's up. You're OK right now because you're near to both your precious family heirlooms. But if I swim off with the locket and leave you to it, you'll find it won't be quite so easy to breathe down here. In fact, by the time I'm out of the lake, I shouldn't think you'll be feeling too good at all." Her pale face loomed up close to Xanthe. "It's all right for me, of course. I don't need either the moonstone *or* the locket to survive underwater. It's one of the many advantages of being a Hexing Witch. But as you know, I would quite *like* to have them both."

Still holding Xanthe by one shoulder, she loosened her scarf and fingered the locket round her neck. "So why don't you do the sensible thing and hand over the moonstone? Then I'll return the favour by taking you back up to the surface. After all, it's one thing to lose your powers as a True Witch, but quite another to lose your *life*."

Xanthe willed her quaking body to recover. She needed to get a grip on herself. "OK," she said. "You win. You can have the moonstone."

Donna blinked back at her. "Excellent," she said, struggling to keep the surprise out of her voice. "I knew you'd see sense in the end. So where is it, then?"

Xanthe undid her coat and began tugging at the zip on her skirt pocket. "It's in here. It seems to have got itself stuck…"

"*I'll* do it," snapped Donna, swooping down and grabbing hold of the zip. "Get your hands out of the way!"

Xanthe didn't need telling twice. She lifted up her arms and in one swift movement seized the chain from round Donna's neck and pulled the locket over her bent head.

Donna let go of the zip and jerked back up, clawing at the chain and sending it spinning out of both girls' reach.

The locket drifted downwards, a silvery flash amidst the grey.

They dived for it as one. Donna hurled herself against Xanthe, trying to push her away, but Xanthe held her course, kicking out with all her strength.

She lunged towards the locket and her fingers closed around it. The next moment she was powering up towards the surface of the lake – one fist curled round the locket, the other stretched out in front of her, poised to punch a hole through the ice with a strength she only now knew she possessed.

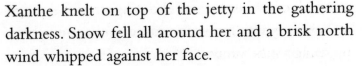

Xanthe knelt on top of the jetty in the gathering darkness. Snow fell all around her and a brisk north wind whipped against her face.

Donna had been right about the cold. She'd felt it the moment she had surfaced from the lake. She staggered to her feet and stumbled down the jetty towards the thicket of trees.

Getting out of the lake had been easier than she'd expected. As she'd neared the surface, the underwater struts of the jetty had loomed into view through the grey water, and she'd managed to smash a hole in the ice close enough to the narrow platform to reach out and touch it. A few moments later and she'd been heaving herself up on to it, dripping wet and shivering with cold.

A noise behind her had her twisting round. Donna was crouching on the end of the jetty, her face contorted with anger.

Xanthe turned back towards the thicket.

Don't let her distract you. Just run and keep on running…

Clenching her fist even more tightly round the locket, she cleared the jetty and sprinted past the boathouse into the shadow of the trees.

She heard Donna clattering down the wooden boards towards her, gaining with every step…

…and then she let out a sharp cry.

A bolt of white heat was shooting straight through her, electrifying her entire body and sending her sprawling to the ground.

Even as it hit her, she knew what it was. There was nothing to show for it this time: no special sign to tell her what was going on. But then this was different, wasn't it? It wasn't some object that was being hexed: it was her.

Around her everything was starting to blur, but inside her head an image was taking shape, an image of Donna standing in line in the playground after the fire alarm had gone off, her face a deathly white.

It's in our nature to fear fire, Grandma Alice had said. *It's in our genes.*

Her body still throbbing with the pain of the hex, Xanthe pulled herself upright and turned towards Donna.

She was standing not far off, completely still, her eyes burning into Xanthe.

Xanthe swallowed. She knew exactly what she had to do. She knew it with every fibre of her being. It was just that it involved the one thing that truly terrified her.

Steadying her breathing, she forced herself to stare back at Donna. Any moment another hex would be blasting through her. If she was going to do this, she needed to do it now.

"I am Xanthe Fox," she murmured, her gaze still fixed on Donna. "I am a True Witch. You cannot stop me from being who I am."

The locket was growing warm in her hand and inside her skirt pocket the moonstone began pulsing with a steady, gentle heat. And then something small and bright sprang from nowhere above the snow-covered ground and flickered between them: a tiny orange flame.

Xanthe's heart raced. Every instinct in her

screamed at her to run, but on the other side of the quivering flame she could see the concentration slip from Donna's eyes and fear lodge in its place.

"I am Xanthe Fox," she repeated to herself. "I am a True Witch."

The flame grew, spreading outwards and upwards until it was leaping into the wintry darkness and licking at the overhanging branches of a nearby tree, spurred on by the stiffening wind.

Donna took a step backwards – but still Xanthe held her gaze. If she looked away even for a second the flame would vanish…

And then the fire took hold, engulfing the tree in a blaze of orange and red.

Donna let out an ear-splitting scream. She turned and hurtled back towards the lake, making for the path that led round it to the back gates of the park.

Xanthe sank to the ground, the air around her thick with the stench of smoke.

She crouched there, her cheeks numb to the sting of falling ash, not moving until the scream was nothing but an echo in her head, and Donna had disappeared into the dusk.

17.
A True Witch

Xanthe crawled backwards, her heart still battering against her chest. She had tried standing up twice already, but both times she had fallen back down, unable to control the trembling in her legs.

She fixed her eyes on the snowy ground. Whatever else she did, she mustn't look up. It was bad enough listening to the fire as the wind tugged it through the thicket towards the lake. She didn't want to have to look at it as well.

She reached the place where she and Donna had grappled with each other earlier. By the eerie light of the flames she could just make out a small dark object lying in the snow, a little way to her right.

It was her phone! It must have dropped out of her pocket during their tussle. She pulled it towards her and glanced around, wondering whether she might strike lucky and find Saul's mobile, too. But she couldn't see any sign of it. Most likely it was lying at the bottom of the lake, covered in weeds and mud.

Still edging backwards, she checked her messages.

Her eyes widened. Grace had texted her six times!

Why haven't you phoned me? demanded the first message. *We need to talk!*

Phone me NOW!!! exclaimed the second. *WHERE ARE YOU?*

Xanthe smiled to herself as she continued to scroll down the texts. Having Grace's words yell out at her from the screen like this was the next best thing to having her right here beside her, and already she could feel the strength returning to her limbs.

She scanned the final message and pulled herself to her feet. Turning her back on the flames, she stumbled through the trees towards the open area of the park and rang Grace.

She answered at once.

"Xanthe! Thank goodness! I was getting really worried. Are you all right?"

"Yeah … I'm OK."

"Are you sure? You don't sound it. Where are you?"

Xanthe stopped short at the edge of the thicket. People were running through the front gates, shouting and pointing.

"I *said*, where are you?"

She shrank back under the cover of the trees and began skirting the thicket to her left. If she could just find the little wooded path that led to the side gate, she might manage to slip away unnoticed.

"*Xanthe?*"

"Oh – er – I've just gone out for a walk, that's all."

"A *walk*? At this time? Have you gone mad or something? It's dark, in case you hadn't noticed. And it's *snowing!*"

Xanthe found the path and turned down it. "I know it is," she muttered, her teeth chattering. "But I've been stuck in the house all day. I needed a bit of fresh air." She hated lying to Grace, but what else could she say? "So what was it you wanted to tell me, then?"

Grace gave a theatrical sigh.

"Kelly's only gone and confessed to Mr Maguire that it was her who set off the fire alarm," she said. "Apparently a new dinner lady saw her heading towards the music wing just before the fire alarm went off. She was too shy to come forward at first, but when she realized how serious the situation was, she decided to report it, so Kelly had no choice but to own up. She won't admit to the other stuff that's happened this week, and she's still swearing blind she didn't take the locket, but she's in so much trouble anyway, it doesn't really matter."

Xanthe hurried towards the side gate. If she didn't know Kelly better, she might almost feel sorry for her. Glancing over her shoulder, she saw that the fire had now reached the boathouse: flames were dancing up its thin wooden sides and curling towards the roof.

"And *then*," Grace went on, "*I* got called in to see Mr Maguire."

"*You* did? But why?"

"He thought I might know why Kelly had it in for you so badly. He reckoned I might be able to explain things to him."

Xanthe reached the gate and let herself on to the narrow street on the other side. "And what did you say?"

"I told him about Kelly being jealous of your trophy at Prize Night. And about your speech in front of Mr Wood and the argument outside the lockers and what happened later on in art. And then I explained how we thought Kelly had copied your handwriting in maths and swapped over the samples in science. Oh, and how she almost certainly took your locket when you were doing the hockey trials."

"I see," said Xanthe. She turned up the hill towards home, ducking as a passer-by stopped and stared at her. What with her matted hair and soaking clothes she must look a complete sight. "Did he – did he say anything about me being allowed back to school?"

"He said he'd be ringing your parents this afternoon. And that he was looking forward to welcoming you back on Monday." Grace paused for breath before rushing on. "And the *totally* fantastic news is that I've been asking around and everyone's now feeling really guilty about cancelling on you and messing up your party. They all want to come over to your place tomorrow to help you celebrate."

"Including Saul?"

"Including Saul. Though he says he's going to have to check with you first to see if you actually *want* him to come. He says he's ready to do some serious grovelling."

Xanthe grinned to herself. She reckoned she could handle a bit of serious grovelling from Saul.

"Anyway, everyone you originally invited says they're up for it. The only person I haven't managed to speak to so far is Donna. She shot off so fast after school I didn't get a chance to ask her."

"Right," said Xanthe faintly. "Well, let's not worry too much about her, shall we? It sounds like there are more than enough people coming already." There was a wail of fire engines in the distance and she put on a burst of speed. "I've got to go, Grace. Thanks for letting me know about Kelly. And for sorting out tomorrow, too. You're the best friend ever."

She crossed the road at the top of the hill and turned right towards Hawthorne Close.

Before she went home there was somebody she badly wanted to see.

Grandma Alice handed Xanthe a mug of steaming hot chocolate and sat down opposite her.

"I still can't quite believe it," she said. "There I was breathing a great big sigh of relief that you were down at the park getting the locket back from Saul, and all the while you were locked in mortal combat with a Hexing Witch. It's almost too much to take in."

Xanthe sipped her hot chocolate. She would never forget the look on her great-grandmother's face when she'd opened the door to her fifteen minutes before. As for what she'd said when she'd learned what had happened – well, she didn't think she'd ever heard such colourful language.

"And to think you defended yourself just as Ethelfreda did," went on Grandma Alice. "To think you actually summoned fire!" She shook her head. "Really, Xanthe, I can't get over how brilliant you've been."

Xanthe blushed. Sitting here right now, still tingling from the bath Grandma Alice had run for her, and dressed in clothes warm from the dryer, the events of the past hour seemed like they'd taken place a lifetime ago.

"You might have told me about the breathing-underwater thing," she said. "Being trapped beneath the ice like that, thinking I was about to drown, was pretty terrifying."

"I would have got round to telling you about it sooner or later," retorted her great-grandmother. "I just didn't think you'd need to know *today*."

"What d'you think will happen to Donna now? Do you reckon she'll be there at school on Monday?"

Grandma Alice shrugged. "Who knows? I expect she'll have no choice. She can hardly tell her parents what went on, can she?"

The phone rang in the kitchen and she got up to answer it.

"That was your mother," she said when she returned. "She's going to be a bit longer with my shopping than she thought." Her lips twitched. "She says the traffic round the park has ground to a complete standstill, and it's heaving with fire engines. Not that we'd know anything about that, would we?"

Xanthe grinned.

"She tried ringing you at home to let you know and when you didn't answer she reckoned you'd most likely come over here. Oh, and she says she's had a very apologetic call on her mobile from the headmaster. Grace was right: you've definitely been let off the hook, so it seems all is forgiven at home. Your mum said she was going to talk to you about getting your party back on track."

Xanthe took another sip of hot chocolate.

Some things were sorting themselves out very nicely indeed. Tomorrow evening would be fun, whatever happened – and with any luck she'd have made up with Saul again by then as well. It was also a big relief to know she could go back to school next week: she'd have missed Grace like anything if she hadn't been allowed to return. It sounded like Kelly wouldn't be causing her any more bother, either. After what had happened with the fire alarm, she'd almost certainly be keeping a very low profile.

She wasn't so sure about Donna, though. True, she'd given her a pretty massive fright down there by the lake, and it might take her a few days to recover, but she was bound to be back at school on Monday – and who knew what trouble she'd try causing once the dust had settled.

Xanthe set down her mug and reached into her skirt pocket.

At least now she had the tools to fight back with. And she'd proved to herself she had the skills needed to deal with Donna's hexes.

She opened the locket and ran her finger over the oval of moonstone that lay snugly inside. She hadn't dared put it on in case Mum came bursting in on them with the shopping and noticed it. It might have led to a few too many awkward questions. She'd have to keep it hidden over the weekend, and then pretend it had turned up in Lost Property on Monday.

"You'll fit that photo I gave you inside it when you get home, won't you?" said Grandma Alice. "I'll rest easier once everything's been set up properly. Besides, it'll make you feel like a proper True Witch."

Xanthe smiled back at her, the locket still nestled in the palm of her hand.

"After the day I've had, I feel like one of those already," she said. "Donna had better watch out – she's definitely met her match."

Also available:

The Boy Who Fell Down Exit 43

Harriet Goodwin

For a millionth of a second the car grazed the drenched moorland. If it had come down on any other patch of ground Finn would simply have been another statistic. Death by dangerous driving. But the car hit the surface of the Earth at Exit 43.

... And at that moment, though no one yet knew it, the entire future of the Underworld changed course.

Finn Oliver knows he'll never come to terms with his father's death, but joy-riding over the moors in his mum's beat-up old car is a quick fix of freedom and forgetting.

Until the accident happens and Finn finds himself hurtling through the wafer-thin divide between the worlds of the living and the dead...

* * *

Harriet Goodwin

GRAVENHUNGER

Unlock the ghostly secret...

Phoenix gasped. How could she have kept a place like this a secret? It was huge. Four storeys of dark grey stone glowering down at them through a multitude of mullioned windows.
... The sun had disappeared behind a dense bank of cloud – and above the towering chimneys of Gravenhunger Manor a thin grey rain was falling.

Gravenhunger Manor isn't the only secret Phoenix's mother took with her to the grave. Something terrible happened at the house during her childhood, something for which she never forgave herself. Phoenix is determined to uncover the truth, but as he begins to dig up the past, he finds himself in mortal danger...

For more about the author,
visit her website:

www.harrietgoodwinbooks.com